She enjoyed being with him—too much!

Nicola tried to act carefree as she dropped down to the warm grass. Keith was watching her intensely in his familiar teasing, enigmatic way.

"Tell me—" he put up a hand to twirl a long strand of her dark hair around his fingers "—would it worry you if you never went back to England?" His voice was lazy. "There's no special man you're missing?"

"I told you," she said very low, "no—"

"In that case...." Suddenly his tone was tinged with excitement and urgency. He made to draw her close, but she sprang to her feet.

She was trembling, but whether from anger or his nearness, she wasn't sure. How *could* he, loving Annabel as he did, try to make love with her now?

GLORIA BEVAN
is also the author of these
Harlequin Romances

Many of these titles are available at your local bookseller.

For a free catalogue listing all available Harlequin Romances
and Harlequin Presents, send your name and address to:

HARLEQUIN READER SERVICE,
M.P.O. Box 707, Niagara Falls, NY 14302
Canadian address: Stratford, Ontario N5A 6W2

Half a World Away

by

GLORIA BEVAN

Harlequin Books

TORONTO • LONDON • LOS ANGELES • AMSTERDAM
SYDNEY • HAMBURG • PARIS • STOCKHOLM • ATHENS • TOKYO

Original hardcover edition published in 1980
by Mills & Boon Limited

ISBN 0-373-02377-4

Harlequin edition published January 1981

CHAPTER ONE

NICOLA bent to move her suitcase a little further from the road edge where the Maori bus driver had placed it. A slim girl with long dark hair blowing in the breeze and an anxious expression in her eyes, she stood watching the vehicle until it vanished around a bend in the highway ahead.

Idiot! To have dismounted from the bus at the wrong stopping place! That was what came of finding oneself a stranger in this unfamiliar New Zealand countryside. She had caught sight of a place name on a road sign — Waihi — why, that was her destination, and had immediately dismounted from the vehicle, only to realise that this wasn't a town at all. There wasn't a building in sight, nothing but acres and acres of spreading farmlands with their grazing cattle. She realised now that the road sign had indicated the name of a district. There was nothing for it but to wait here at the roadside for the next bus to come along, and goodness only knew when that would be. Right at this moment, she vowed, she would be glad of an offer of a lift into town in any vehicle at all, with any old driver at all who happened along the empty road.

The next moment she had second thoughts in the matter, for a long truck was pulling to a stop at her side and the oddest-looking man she had seen in a long while was thrusting his head from the cab. Not that she could glimpse much of him, the thoughts ran through her mind, not beneath the shapeless felt hat, stained and motheaten and pulled so low over his eyes that she could glimpse no more than the lower portion of a tanned masculine face.

'Want a lift, lady? I'm going into town, so jump in!'

She hesitated, something about his voice checking the denial that trembled on her lips. Deep, vibrant, with an attractive timbre, it wasn't at all the type of voice that matched the clothing he wore. He looked such a disreput-able-looking character—that awful hat! In spite of the unexpectedly cultured tones, she decided to play for safety.

'No, thank you.' Even to her own ears her voice held a prim, superior inflection. 'There'll be a bus along to Waihi at any minute now, I expect.'

'You've got to be lucky. Sorry, miss,' did she imagine an ironic tinge in the deep tones, 'but you're in for a long wait. There won't be a bus through this way until tomorrow morning.'

'Oh!' If only she could see his face more clearly. If only it wasn't for that frightful hat! He was an odd-looking character, very. On the other hand he was evidently a worker in the employ of the firm whose name she could see printed along the side of the truck: Lorimer Timber Company. All at once she decided to throw caution to the winds.

His hand was on the starter and clearly he was losing patience with her. 'Please yourself.'

'Wait, I'm coming!'

In a flash he had leaped down from the cab, a tall man wearing a thick crumpled jacket. A woollen jacket in this heat of early summer? The garment appeared to be a little on the small side for his wide shoulders. Nicola took in the rough slacks, the mud-caked boots. Irrelevantly, she noticed too the shapely, sunbrowned hand as he tossed her suitcase into the back of the truck.

As she climbed up into the high seat of the cab, she was glad of the neat black pants suit she had purchased in a London fashion store in expectation of this trip out to New Zealand. The next moment he had climbed in be-side her and flung shut the heavy door.

As he put the truck into gear she found herself staring down at his ankles and resisting a wild impulse to giggle, for the heavy stained slacks were caught around the ankles with lengths of twine. Who would have believed that she would actually meet up with a man wearing, what was the term for the old-fashioned ties, bowyangs? The New Zealand male must indeed be antiquated in his choice of working gear. And that was odd, she mused, remembering that during her short stopover in Auckland on her arrival from London, the men she had passed by in the bright attractive streets had appeared to her little different from the menfolk back home, except of course for their deeply tanned skins that lent them a certain toughness. It passed through her mind too that from the window of the airport bus that had taken her to the city she had noticed a number of workmen engaged on construction work on a span of a bridge over a river. The deeply bronzed men had been clad in cool shorts and shirts. On well—she gave up trying to solve the puzzle—maybe here in the country district, farmers wore a different type of working gear.

At least, this man did. A pang of apprehension shot through her as she took in the empty road ahead. What had she done? But it was too late to change her mind about travelling with him to town, if indeed he were bound for the town. Already they were moving along the wide bitumen highway.

In an effort to banish her misgivings she said quickly—too quickly; would he notice her nervousness, 'I see by the name outside that this is a timber truck. There's no timber in it now, though,' she heard herself babbling on. 'There's enough room in the back for a dozen suitcases, but there's nothing there except,' she glanced back over her shoulder through a small window behind her, 'my case and a pick. Is it yours?'

She looked up at the masculine face beside her, but that horrible hat still hid his expression. Did country workers in this country wear hats all of the time, and ancient moth-eaten models at that?

His gaze was on the straight stretch of roadway ahead. 'Just for today. I borrowed it specially.'

'Whatever for?' If she kept the conversation to ordinary topics, nothing personal——

He jerked his head in the direction of the bush-clad slopes rising behind them. 'I've been out doing a bit of prospecting, digging for gold in them thar hills. Hasn't anyone ever told you that Waihi is a goldmining town?'

'Oh yes, I know.' Hadn't she borrowed books from the local library and studied the history of New Zealand, ever since she knew she was making the trip out here? Especially had she learned all she could of the mining district of Waihi. Gazing towards the green slopes rising around them, she said smugly, 'Who would believe that in the old gold rush days there was more gold found in these hills than in any other place in the world?'

'True.'

'But I didn't realise that people were still trying to find gold here, and with a pick!'

'You'd be surprised what goes on around here.' Did she imagine a faintly ironic note in the surprisingly attractive voice? 'Oh yes, there's gold buried in these hills, silver too. All you need is the know-how to get it out.'

And he had used a pick! For something to say she asked brightly: 'Did you have any luck with your prospecting? Find anything worthwhile?'

For a moment he was silent. 'Let's say it was worth the effort.' Once again she suspected an ironic note in the voice that seemed so cultured for this unkempt-looking timber worker. He added carelessly, 'You never know what you might pick up, once you start looking around.'

She hoped he didn't mean what she suspected he did.

'You mean metals? Gold, silver?'

'And other things.' If only she could glimpse his expression—but his deadpan voice gave nothing away.

She forced a laugh that even to her ears sounded anything but jolly and carefree, 'I hope you don't mean me,' and could have kicked herself for the betraying quaver in her voice.

'Why should I mean you?'

'Well ...' Her voice trailed away. As well as being apprehensive, she was now feeling embarrassed. There seemed no suitable answer to his question, so she turned her head aside and stared hard at the green paddocks flashing by.

As they went on in silence Nicola tried to concentrate on her surroundings, her gaze taking in an occasional sprawling, red-roofed farmhouse with its shelterbelt of tall trees, and always the hazy blue hills in the distance. With a sense of relief she realised they must be approaching the city, for they were passing other traffic on the road, Land Rovers and farm trucks, a red tractor and big, dust-spattered cars. And everywhere the clear bright sunshine lent a sparkle to trees and the green, green grass.

Strange, she mused, to come so abruptly to another hemisphere, to leave the chill of an English winter for early summer skies of this tender blue. Her thoughts drifted back to a neat brick villa in Lincolnshire, the only home she had known since the time when as a small child she had been left an orphan and Aunt Bella, a childless widow, had taken Nicola into her heart and her home. Could it be only a few short weeks since the momentous day when after a dispiriting day at the office where she worked, she had hurried home through driving rain to be greeted at the door by an excited Aunt Bella.

'I thought you were never coming! I can't wait to tell you! I've just had the most marvellous idea. I've been thinking about it all day.' A pause, then dramatically, triumphantly, 'How would you like to take a trip out to New Zealand, all expenses paid? I mean it,' for Nicola mopping her rain-wet hair with a towel, was eyeing her aunt in amused disbelief.

'But I do!' Small, stout and well-corseted, Aunt Bella followed Nicola into her bedroom. 'I've had this plan in my mind for ages, but today I made up my mind. You see, it arrived today, the legacy I've been waiting for from Cousin Jim's estate, and this is something I really want to do with the windfall—to send you out to New Zealand. I've been on the phone to the travel agency,' she ran on in the high sweet tones that always seemed to Nicola so youthful for a woman of her aunt's years, 'and it seems there's an economy fare that will give you two months over there. That should give you time to find out something, that is if there is anything to find out about your Uncle Walter. Sometimes I wonder if he's still alive, but all the same, I'd just like to *know*. Even if you don't have any luck with your enquiries, and you never find a trace of him, at least I'll have the satisfaction of knowing that I've done my best to locate him. And you'll have had a holiday—well, a second summer, a sort of holiday.'

Nicola, sorting through a drawer for dry garments, could scarcely believe her ears. At last she turned and said slowly, 'It's wonderful of you to think of it, but I wouldn't dream of spending your money, just like that, for nothing. I'd feel mean about it for a start. It's good of you to offer me the chance, but I just couldn't think of it.'

'Of course you could, and anyway, it wouldn't be for nothing. It would mean a lot to me to have you take on this little job of work. And I'll tell you another thing,' as Nicola opened her lips to protest, 'if you don't have a go at it I'll hire someone out there in New Zealand to do it. There must be agencies there who would be quite used to tracing missing people.'

Aunt Bella went on thoughtfully, 'It seems so strange. Somehow I can't believe that Walter is still alive or he would have written to me. Yet he might still be living over there in New Zealand all these years. I'd just like to *know*. After all, he is my only brother.' Nicola had heard Uncle Walter's life history, or what anyone knew of it, many times, and scarcely listened as the high sweet voice ran on. 'No word at all in all that time. There was that one letter written from the opal fields in Western Australia saying he would be leaving there before long, and would write me from the new address. With only the two of us in the family, you'd have thought he would have kept in touch. But of course Walter was never what you'd call a *dependable* sort of person. As a boy he was always in some scrape or other and when he grew up he wouldn't stick at a job for more than a few weeks. He was always wanting to rush off to some foreign place. He always had an idea that somehow, some way, he'd find a way of making a lot of money quickly, without having to work for it. I do hope he changed his ideas.'

For a moment a worried expression crossed Aunt Bella's plump, pleasant face. 'He got into a spot of trouble once or twice, nothing serious really, though there was some talk about a big sum of money going missing once while he was staying at a friend's place for a weekend. Fortunately it was all hushed up, and anyway,' she recovered her cheerful outlook, 'it was probably just a momentary temptation. Walter never meant half of the wild things he said.'

'What sort of things?' Nicola had changed into a dry warm skirt and her voice came muffled as she pulled a knitted sweater over her head.

'Oh, he was a great talker, Walter was. Always going on about some wild scheme or other. He used to make imaginary plans about robbing a bank and all those sort of ridiculous things—but of course it didn't really *mean* anything. He was far too nice a person to do anything like that. It was just talk and high spirits.' She took from her pocket a sepia-coloured card. 'This is all he ever sent me from New Zealand, this postcard from the place with the odd name. It isn't even a pretty picture, just an ugly-looking old goldmine battery.'

Nicola had come to peer over her aunt's shoulder. 'Maybe it was interesting to him. It must have meant something to him at the time. He could have worked in the battery.'

'It's possible. If only men would write more details on their postcards!' Aunt Bella sighed. 'Just a few scribbled words: "Have left West Australia and have decided to try my luck in New Zealand. I'll let you know my new address when I get a permanent place to stay here."'

Nicola picked up a comb and ran it through her long dark hair. 'But he never did let you know?'

'No. I wrote three times to him at this Waihi place in New Zealand, but the letters were all returned to me, address unknown. Oh well, you never can tell. He might have moved on. He could have married a girl and settled somewhere nearby. Some of the family could still be living out there in New Zealand.'

Nicola regarded her aunt laughingly. 'He doesn't sound to me the sort of man to settle anywhere! And there must be lots of people by that name who have no connection with him. There could be oodles of Fletchers, even out there on the other side of the world.'

Aunt Bella's small plump hand waved aside Nicola's objections. 'Now don't start making difficulties! I've got the money to spare and this happens to be something I really want to spend it on. If I didn't have this stupid lame leg I'd be taking off on the Air New Zealand plane myself. I even thought of doing that for a while, but I know I'd get all worn out before I even got started. You might have to follow the trail a bit, get around the country, but your legs are a lot younger and stronger than mine. Besides, I want you to have the trip.'

'You really mean it, don't you?' For the first time the fantastic plan was taking on reality in Nicola's mind. 'You don't mind spending all that money?'

'Cheap at the price, I'd say! If you don't find out something about Walter, a trained secretary like you, no one could. I'm in the market for someone to do the work and you're the one I'd choose. Now stop trying to think up objections. You know my friend Meg who lives up in Scotland? She's been longing to come and stay with me for ages and this will work in nicely. And if you're thinking about the office, I had a word over the phone with your boss, just a few minutes before you got home——'

Nicola gasped, 'You—what?'

'He was most helpful, said he was quite happy for you to take a couple of months' leave of absence from the office. That's why,' Aunt Bella stated calmly, 'you're so ideal for the job of going overseas. No parents to hold you back because of health or age, no husband to start throwing his weight about—and they do, you know, when wives get a chance to take off alone and enjoy themselves. And I couldn't afford to pay two fares.' Aunt Bella, who was apt to wander off the subject momentarily, swept on. 'But luckily for me, you're still single. I don't know why really,' she murmured thoughtfully, 'when you're so pretty —Now don't look at me like that! It's not just my opinion, everyone says the same! Anyway, it's just wonderful for me you're being free to please yourself and go where you want to—Heavens,' she broke off, sniffing the air, 'the raspberry pie! It's boiling over!' From half way down the tiny hall her voice floated back to Nicola. 'Think about it.'

Nicola went on thinking about her supposed 'freedom'. How horrified the dear would be were she to know that it was Aunt Bella herself, with her lameness, her inability to move alone any distance from her own home, who was the real stumbling block in that respect. Nicola knew that had it not been for love and gratitude, and a niggling conscience, she would have left the Lincolnshire village long ago to seek work in a city. In London perhaps. Somewhere where she could enjoy the companionship of others of her own age group and, now that she could support herself, revel in the independence of renting a flat of her own.

Not that she minded staying on in the village, working as secretary to a solicitor in the same small office where she had been employed ever since leaving business college. It had been wonderfully good of her aunt to take her in when Nicola was little and helpless and alone in the world. How could she leave her now? Not that Aunt Bella would hesitate for a moment were she to be aware of Nicola's feelings in the matter, but all the same ... Nevertheless, except for the restlessness, the feeling of frustration that had assailed her so often of late, she was happy enough here—well, most of the time.

As to the husband bit, she couldn't understand herself any more than could her aunt, but there it was. There was no man friend she cared about particularly, and the odd thing about it was that there never had been. Nicola puzzled over the matter.

You couldn't help knowing when you looked attractive and perhaps she had been lucky in having been born with a heart-shaped face, eyes of an intense dark blue, and soft dark hair that did what you wanted it to. Given all that, wouldn't you think that at the ripe old age of twenty-one ('and so pretty') you would have had one deep-down, once-in-a-lifetime romance? When you came right down to it, her love life, if you could call it that, had been no more

than a succession of forgettable romances into which she had
drifted in and out without any real depth of feeling. As to the
fires of love and consuming passion that made everything else
in life pale into insignificance, such emotions weren't for her.
Maybe she just wasn't built that way, and yet... Her eyes
were dreamy.

Wouldn't you imagine that fate would have arranged
things differently? Fate, or herself? Could it be because in
the permissive world of today she happened to be a girl with
old-fashioned ideas? She didn't have that small square chin
for nothing. A girl with her own loyalties and convictions that
didn't always go along with today's standards, like staying
here at home with Aunt Bella instead of branching out, finding work that was more to her taste, running her own flat in
London, being her own woman. Well, she couldn't help it.
That was just her!

So much for freedom. But now, all at once, excitement
stirred in her. For two whole months she would be gloriously
free. She had longed to travel overseas, but if it had not been
for Aunt Bella, her meagre savings would never have stretched to cover a trip to the other side of the world. Now everything was changed. Fate had handed her this journey to new
surroundings, fresh interests — perhaps, even, a new romance. The real thing at last? Who knows? Maybe, beneath
faraway southern stars, there waited for her a man with
whom she could *really* fall in love. And even if she could find
no trace of Uncle Walter, the trip would be, as Aunt Bella
had said, a kind of holiday.

'So you're a new arrival in this country?' The resonant
tones jerked her head to the present.

She glanced up at a portion of sunbrowned cheek and a
strongly moulded masculine chin. 'How did you guess?'

'It sticks out a mile. The labels on your suit case tell a story
for a start. The funny way you say "Wai-hi",' he flicked her a
sideways glance. 'And I'll tell you something else. You don't
often come across a girl with a skin like yours in this part of
the world. Our grandfathers had a name for it, I believe.
Peaches and cream?'

'Beetroot red, more likely, in this hot sun!' But her

apprehension deepened. If he was going to get personal, goodness knew where his interest would end. She was aware of his glance and felt the hot colour rising in her cheeks. Now she really was beetroot colour!

His eyes returned to the road and he swung out to pass a long silver milk tanker. 'You've come quite a way to be in on the festivities here.' His tone was so matter-of-fact that she gave a sigh of relief and relaxed against the back of the seat. Maybe the peaches and cream bit wasn't so personal after all. Her imagination seemed to be working overtime today. 'Must have meant a lot to you, to bring you all this way.'

Before she could make an answer he went on, 'Most of the tourists who come out to Kiwi-land are bound for the attractions they read about in the travel brochures. Those spectacular splendours of the South Island are really something. Or if they hit the North, they go for the boiling mudpools and geysers of Rotorua, or take off for one of the big game fishing spots in the Bay of Islands.'

'I'm not exactly a tourist.'

They were moving along a wide highway lined with towering palm trees and all at once they swept by a motel sign. Had Nicola caught sight of the notice in time she would have asked him to drop her there, but of course there would be other accommodation places where she could put up. A private hotel perhaps?

He seemed to tune in on her thoughts. 'Got somewhere jacked up to stay?'

'No—well,' all at once she remembered the letter of introductions tucked away in her leather shoulder bag, 'I have in a way.' It had been given to her by her employer. 'Bill Hazlett's a friend of mine,' he had told her with interest. 'We were at school together, then later he went out to New Zealand and married there. He and his wife live in Waihi. It's a family home and her family have been there for a couple of generations. Bill has a son who took up law too. Not that I see much of Bill these days, but we correspond and I had a trip out to see him and his family five years ago. You mightn't want to make use of this,' he had handed her a handwritten note, 'but you never know, you might find it useful if things come unstuck. Sometimes it helps to know someone in a town.'

Nicola had thanked him and thought no more about the matter. She had no intention of using the introduction just now. If she did have to fall back on it as a last resort, she would find out if it were convenient for the Hazletts to have her, before forcing herself on their hospitality.

'You've got friends in town, then?' he persisted. 'They'll be able to put you up?'

'Oh yes.'

'Good! If you hadn't, I wouldn't give much for your chances. With the celebrations on, every hotel and motel in the place is booked out for the next two weeks.'

'Oh!' Something of her apprehension must have got through to him, for his tone had softened. 'Except at Sky Lodge, that is. It's a bit out of the way—look, you can see it from here.' She followed his gaze towards a pine-covered hill that towered into a translucent blue sky. 'That's it, the old white place almost at the summit.' She caught a glimpse of a blur of white against the sombre green of surrounding pine plantations. The next minute they swung around a bend and the dwelling was lost to view.

'It's not so handy to what's happening in the town,' he was saying. 'A bit isolated in a way, but there's always transport in to the city of one sort or another. And there's swags of room. Not exactly a five-star luxury job, but all the same——'

That was the moment when she heard herself saying eagerly, hopefully, 'Maybe I could stay there, then?'

'It's up to you. Like I said, it's a fair step out of town but when it comes to any port in a storm——'

She fell right into the trap. 'Could you take me there then, now? You seem to know it well.'

'Should do.' His voice was deadpan. 'I happen to live there.'

'I see.' She sought wildly in her mind for words and at last came up with: 'It's awfully good of you to offer but, if it's so far out of town, I might be better off to stay with ... my friends ... after all.' Were the people to whom she carried an introductory letter any nearer to the town? She hoped so. If only she had taken the trouble to find out. On an inspiration she added, 'You see, they'll be expecting me.' No need to add a qualifying 'some time'. She had no idea whether the strangers had yet received a letter mentioning her name from her employer.

'Tremendous! You've got somewhere to go, then!' To her surprise he appeared to be immensely relieved at her decision. Was it possible that he had been merely trying to help her, a stranger in town? Oh dear, if only she hadn't got herself involved with this unknown man.

She had planned to book in at an accommodation place for a week until she could make other arrangements. Now he had informed her that owing to the special celebrations being held in the town this week, finding somewhere to stay would be out of the question, and somehow, in spite of his off-putting appearance, she felt inclined to believe him.

All at once she realised that they were moving along a suburban street lined with timber houses painted in gay pastel colourings and set far back from the street. Sweeping lawns surrounded the dwellings and flowering bushes were everywhere. A little further on there were villas of an earlier era, standing alongside modern ranch-style houses. They then swept around a corner to come in sight of a wide tree-lined street. From the old-time and modern stores on either side of the highway, banners unfurled in the breeze and strings of flags fluttered their gay colours overhead. Faintly in the distance came the echo of band music.

'You're just in time to see the procession. May as well take a look.' The man braked to a stop amongst a cluster of parked vehicles on the road and they got out of the truck to join the crowd of onlookers who were gathered on the street corner. He turned to her with a grin. 'Your first experience of the Goldfields Centenary Celebrations!'

So that, she mused, was what the festivities were all about. The next moment she forgot everything else as a sound of cheering rose around them and to the beat of a drum, the local brass band went marching by. Close behind came the Master of the Hunt, followed by hounds and the hunt. Then a team of bullocks went plodding past them. 'The driver is a genuine "bullocky",' her companion told her, 'possibly the only one left in the country.' Nicola, however, was fascinated by a group of Maori girls who from the shelter of a fern-lined whare were smiling and waving to the crowd. As the long truck with its greenery went past, Nicola waved enthusiastically in return. The long dark tresses of the Maori girls were caught back from their faces with woven headbands and the girls wore their native costumes of bodice and skirts of flax woven in the red, white and black taniko pattern. Nicola was straining for a last glimpse of the truck when an ancient fire engine approached, firemen with hoses and buckets lightheartedly spraying a stream of water towards the cheering bystanders.

Nicola waved and laughed with the crowd, but underneath the gaiety her thoughts were whirling. It was true then what the man had told her about a week of celebrations in the town, and that meant she had no option but to fall back on her letter of introduction. When they got back in the truck she took the envelope from her bag and quickly scanned the handwritten note. 'Hazlett,' she told him, 'that's the name of the friends I'm to stay with and they live at——' Once again she consulted the letter.

'It's okay. I know John and his folk. They live no distance from here.'

They were moving along a main highway, then they swung into a suburban street. I like this town, Nicola mused. All the flowers and shrubs and greenery. It's so fresh-looking. The stores look old and somehow interesting and I've never seen such deep ditches on either side of the street. I only hope these Hazlett people will be at home, and that they'll be able to take me in. Otherwise ... She pushed aside the possibility of being forced to accept the hospitality of her companion. It didn't appeal one bit!

'John and I were at school together,' he was saying.

She turned to eye him curiously. 'Really?'

'Now he's my lawyer, and a darn good one he is too. He's saved me a dollar or two over the years and I'm grateful to him. What he doesn't know about taxes and property isn't worth knowing.'

His lawyer! Nicola was more than ever mystified. Why would he need the services of a lawyer, a man like this? Why, he spoke almost as if he were a man of property, this odd-looking character who wore darned, shabby slacks tied around his ankles with twine.

The next moment she forgot the matter, her attention caught by the gracious old stone house on a rise ahead. Through a drift of apple and peach blossom in an old orchard, stone chimneys rose to pierce the blue of the sky.

The man at her side followed her gaze. 'That's it, that's the Hazlett place.'

She leaned forward, enraptured. 'Why, it's just lovely, all so beautifully kept!'

'Should be. It's been in the same family ever since the old gold-rush days. Mrs Hazlett's folk were old identities in the district like a lot of others down this way, including my own parents.'

'But that's wonderful, their having lived here all that time.' Now that she was safely in sight of her destination (and blessedly, the house was close to the town) her qualms fled and the thoughts that were uppermost in her mind tumbled from her lips.

'That's really why I've come here. It's a sort of holiday, or so Aunt Bella says. You see, she gave me the trip out here because she wants me to try to trace her brother. What a hope! Do you know, the last she heard of him was a card posted from Wai-hi,' she spoke the Maori syllables with care, 'and that was years and years ago! After that,' she flung her hands upwards in an expressive gesture, 'nothing. No more letters, not even a postcard. No one knows whether Uncle Walter ever got married or if he stayed on here or not. So my aunt had this idea that she'd send me out to New Zealand to try to dig up something about her brother. I mean, it's different if you're on the spot.'

Now that they were approaching the Hazletts' home, excitement took over and nothing else mattered, certainly not the oddly-garbed man seated at her side. He was just a stranger who had given her a lift into town, someone who had chanced to come along at the moment when she needed help. It was his appearance that had misled her ... that hat. It had made her distrust his motives. Not that it mattered what she thought about him, it wasn't likely she would ever meet up with him again.

The deep vibrant tones broke into her musing. 'You'll be kept pretty busy if you're going to have a go at tracing someone you've lost touch with all that long ago.'

'I know, I know. All I've got to go on is an old post-card and a picture of Uncle Walter as a young man. But I have a few ideas to go on with.'

'Such as?'

'Oh, you know, the usual things people do when they're trying to trace someone. Try and find some old news-papers, take a look through the local telephone book.' She sighed. 'If only Fletcher wasn't such an ordinary name, but still ... I thought of trying to locate some old electoral rolls that I could take a glance through. And I could try and look up the old records at the mine. Seeing he came from the opal fields in Australia he could have worked there.'

'It's possible. The mine was still chugging along at that time. At least you're not up against the usual stumbling block when it comes to finding a missing relative.'

She glanced across at him curiously. 'How do you mean?'

He shrugged. 'Rumours, false reports, all that stuff. You'd be surprised how facts can get distorted over the years. Stories get enhanced until there's very little truth in an incident. A man who came out here twenty years ago might get a reputation amongst his relatives back home in England or America or Canada as a miner who'd struck it rich, that sort of thing.'

She laughed. 'Oh no, there's no story like that about Uncle Walter. With him, according to all reports, it would be something quite different——' She broke off abruptly. There was no need to reveal family secrets, or rather suspicions, of Uncle Walter, to this stranger.

They were moving along a quiet suburban street, passing by the grey stone ruins of what appeared to Nicola to be an old castle standing on a rise. She was about to enquire about the stone ruins when she realised they were approaching a wide entrance with stone pillars on either side. The next moment the man had braked to a stop, but he made no move to get out of the vehicle.

Nicola too was still, looking out beyond the orchard to spacious lawns studded with flowering shrubs. There was yellow broom, some vividly blue flowers that were new to her, the pinks and reds of azaleas and rhododendrons. 'It's like you said,' she was speaking her thoughts aloud, 'you never know what you can find when you look in the right place.'

'It was built for the original owner of the mine and the family have kept the place going ever since.'

Her gaze was on the gracious old house dreaming in the spring sunshine. 'That's just what I've been hoping to find—a family who have been here since the early days of the town. Who knows, they might have some old photographs, newspaper cuttings, records——'

'Could be.' His gaze swept the wide open windows, where filmy white curtains billowed in the breeze. 'Looks like they're at home. You said they were expecting you.' Still he made no move to open the door of the truck. 'I've just had a thought. If you'd like to take in a bit of local colour, I've got double tickets for the centenary ball they're putting on tonight in the local hall. If you'd——'

Her look of indignation must have got through to him, for his slightly off-handed tone changed to one of amused indifference. 'Like that, is it? I'll let you into a secret, Nicola——' Nicola! He must have gleaned the name from her suitcase label. 'I don't always look like this. I've

got some real nice gear up at the house. You'd be surprised how I can get myself up when I want to—No?'
Even without looking directly in his direction she was
aware he was regarding her searchingly, no doubt taking in
her horrified expression. 'Pity. You might have enjoyed the
experience. Another time, maybe.' He reached towards
the door handle.

She eyed him suspiciously, the ridiculous thought crossing her mind that he was having her on, enjoying a private
joke at her expense. If only she could glimpse his expression!

Dropping to the ground, he came around the vehicle
to help her down the high step. Then he picked up her
suitcase and together they strolled up the driveway. She
wondered if he had stopped the truck at the entrance
gates instead of driving up to the house because he wanted
to ask her about the ball tonight. They climbed the
wide steps of the wisteria-screened porch and he put
down her suitcase.

'If you're interested, there's a swag of old-time stuff
stashed away at my place.' 'My place', she thought, was
no doubt a rented room in the big apartment house on
the hill.

'There's an old family scrapbook that's crammed with
newspaper cuttings, photos, all that stuff,' he was saying, 'that might give you some clues. Fletcher, you said
the name was? I'll see if I can dig up anything to help
and if I come across the name, you might care to come
up to Sky Lodge and give it the once-over.'

'Thank you,' she murmured politely, but inwardly, all
her suspicions of him came rushing back. Was he making
it all up to suit his own ends, trying to further the casual
acquaintance? He must be. And yet he sounded sincere
enough.

Before she could make up her mind on the matter he
had turned away, a hand raised in a gesture of farewell.
'Good luck with your prospecting. I hope you get somewhere with it.'

'Me too,' she said in her soft voice, 'and thanks for the lift!'

'Any time.' He had paused on the steps, to glance back over his shoulder. 'I'm always out on the road with the truck. Keith's the name. You can reach me any time at the Sky Lodge. Don't forget!'

She watched him as he took the steps two at a time, then he went striding up the driveway. Despite his definitely odd appearance she had to admit that there was something about him. Even his dreadful garments couldn't altogether disguise the erect back and firm step. Funny, the way he was striding along the path one would imagine he was someone of importance. Maybe he was, in his own small world.

The next moment, pressing her finger to the door bell, she forgot the truck driver. She could hear the muffled sound of door chimes echoing somewhere behind the closed door and all at once she was nervous, horribly so. For two pins she would take to her heels and run down the steps and out to the truck. She could see the driver waiting at the wheel of his vehicle. If she went now, this minute ... She pulled herself back to some degree of composure. For tonight at least she faced a choice between the uncertain hospitality of strangers or ... One thing was for sure, she told herself, and that was that almost any lodging place in the town would be preferable to spending a night at the truck driver's rooming house on the high hill.

'Hello? Did you want to see someone?' The door had opened and she found herself meeting the enquiring gaze of a young man with a serious expression and a rather pedantic manner of speaking. Light was reflected from his gold-rimmed glasses with their thick lenses. 'Can I help you?'

'Yes—no—that is——'

'Come inside anyway!'

As Nicola stepped into a carpeted hallway she was forced to raise her voice above the blaring notes of a stereo echoing above the bursts of talk and laughter from a nearby room. 'I hope I haven't come at an awkward time. You

see, I've got a letter for you.' She fumbled in her shoulder
bag with unsteady fingers and drew out an envelope. 'I've
just arrived in the country, from England ... only got off
the plane in Auckland yesterday.' Her voice died into
silence. Why was she yakking on? Better to give him a
chance to read the letter. It would explain her situation
much better than she could.

He paused to slit open the envelope with a well-tended
hand. As his eyes behind the gold-rimmed glasses skimmed
the handwritten page, she reflected that he was an extremely well-groomed young man. His smooth dark hair was
carefully slicked down over his forehead and his well-
pressed brown slacks and crisp fawn-coloured shirt were
immaculate. Clearly he was a man who took a pride in his
appearance, not like the truck driver.

Apparently he was a slow reader—or could it be, she
wondered, that he was deliberating on whether or not to
take a strange girl into his home? As he glanced up and
she met his welcoming grin, however, she knew she was
certain of lodging for one night at least.

'But this is great news!' His glance was taking in
Nicola's creamy skin and sweetly-curved mouth. 'Your
turning up like this out of the blue—is this all the gear
you've got?' She nodded and he picked up her suitcase.
'Dad will be on top of the world when he knows who you
are. He's always going on about his old buddy over in
Lincolnshire. I'm John, by the way, and you're Miss
Ayres?'

'Nicola.'

'Right, Nicola it is—come along with me and meet the
folks.' He was leading the way down a long carpeted hall
and presently he flung open a door at the end of the passage. Nicola stood motionless, staring into a blur of faces
in the crowded room. At her entrance the buzz of chatter
had died away. Someone in the nearby room had switched
off the stereo music and in the silence she found herself
a centre of attention.

'Meet Miss Nicola Ayres, folks!' The young man with
the measured tones was standing by her side. 'She's come

all the way from England, would you believe?'

Nicola followed his gaze towards a tired-looking man of middle age who was hurrying towards them.

'This is going to rock you, Dad,' John called to his father. 'Nicola comes from Lincolnshire and she's brought a letter from your old mate Dave Mansfield. She works in his office.'

'No!' Nicola's hand was being pumped vigorously by the grey-haired man with the thin intelligent face. He appealed to a small woman with bright brown eyes and bushy hair who had come to join them. 'Joan, tell her she's welcome to stay with us for as long as she likes!'

A little overwhelmed by the unexpected warmth of her welcome, Nicola protested in her soft tones, 'Only if you have room for me. I know you weren't expecting me.'

'We'll always make room for a friend of Dave's.' Mr Hazlett's voice rang with sincerity. 'That's the truth, isn't it, Joan?'

'We'll be delighted for you to stay.' Nicola was aware of the swift appraisal of shrewd dark eyes. 'No use my trying to introduce you to everyone,' Mrs Hazlettt went on. 'There are far too many. They're all friends and relations.'

Nicola nodded and tried to make her smile extend over the faces all turned in her direction.

'Come along, my dear,' Mrs Hazlett was saying, 'and I'll show you where you'll sleep. You won't mind sharing a room just for a couple of nights? John's friend Sharon is staying with us for the weekend. When *she* goes home,' Nicola caught a note of grim satisfaction in the quick tones, 'it will be different.' Clearly, she thought, John's mother would be more than happy when the other girl went away.

'I'm afraid,' she murmured as she went with Mrs Hazlett along a smaller hall, 'that I've come at a busy time.'

'Oh, it's just the celebrations, and all these people aren't staying at the house—goodness no! It's a family gathering here today. After all,' she smiled her thin-lipped smile, 'a centenary of a goldmining town doesn't come along all that often—here we are.' She flung open a door leading into a sunny bedroom and a girl who had been seated on the bed leaped guiltily to her feet.

'I was just ...' To Nicola the other girl's sandy-coloured hair, thin freckled face and light green eyes lent her a curiously colourless look.

'In here, John!' Mrs Hazlett called to the young man, who came into the room to put Nicola's suitcase down on a low table. The next moment Nicola caught the stormy glance between him and Sharon. Whatever the trouble between them at least it had nothing to do with her.

'This is Sharon—Nicola,' Mrs Hazlett spoke briskly as John left the room. 'You two will have to share for a night or so.'

'You might have asked me about it first!' Sharon's voice was tight with resentment, but the older woman took not the slightest notice. She turned towards Nicola.

'Sharon will show you where the bathroom is, and there's lots of hot water if you'd like to take a shower.'

'Thank you, I'd like that.'

When Mrs Hazlett left them alone together, Nicola gazed at the two dressing chests. 'Which one of these can I use?'

The pale-faced girl shrugged her thin shoulders. 'Please yourself.' But Nicola had caught the glint of tears in the light-coloured eyes. In silence she opened a drawer and was relieved to find it empty. Bending over her suitcase and taking out piles of clothing, she was aware, even without looking up, of the other girl's hostile stare. She decided, however, to play for a lighthearted approach. 'I suppose you're wondering where on earth I've sprung from and what I'm doing here, a complete stranger dropping in on you all from nowhere?'

'No.' The word fell into a silence.

Nicola sighed, and taking a nylon wrap from her suitcase threw it on the bed. She tried again. 'I only arrived in the country yesterday on the London plane. Do you know, I actually thought that in Wai-hi I'd be able to find accommodation, no trouble at all.'

'Wai*hi*,' Sharon corrected her in an expressionless tone,

'not Wai-hi, the way you say it.'

Nicola choked back the angry reply that trembled on her lips. After all, the girl did seem to be upset. She forced her voice to calmness. 'Well, whatever it is. When I heard about the celebrations that were on here there was nothing for it but to come here with my letter of introduction. Luckily, I'd brought it along with me. The man in the office where I work happens to be a friend of Mr Hazlett.'

Sharon made no answer. She had drifted to the window and was staring out into the garden outside, nervously twisting the diamond ring on her finger. As she turned her head, once again Nicola caught the shine of unshed tears in the other girl's eyes. Seeing that Sharon had something on her mind it seemed useless trying to be friendly.

Nicola picked up her wrap and a towel and went in search of the bathroom. When she came back after a refreshing shower, she found Sharon lying stretched face down on her bed, eyes downcast and a paperback lying open on the pillow. One swift glance, however, and Nicola had taken in the eyelids reddened with weeping. She said nothing, but busied herself brushing her hair until it shone, then she twisted the long dark strands in a knot and caught it high on her head. Deftly she applied make-up, a touch of pink lipstick, a smear of blue eye-shadow, an upward flick of a mascara wand to her lashes. A pity, she mused, that Sharon didn't take the trouble to darken the colourless eyelashes that did nothing for her pale face. She said nothing, however, and all the time she pulled over her head a dress of soft floral cotton and slipped her feet into woven string sandals, the other girl kept her gaze glued to her book. Oh well, Nicola thought, if she wants to play it that way.

At dinner that evening Nicola gave up trying to sort out the various uncles and aunts, cousins and friends who were gathered around the big table. A shy-looking youth with a red, freshly scrubbed face sat at her side. Of Sharon she could see no sign. As to the food, not in a long time had Nicola been offered such a choice of tempting dishes.

There were plates of pâtés and appetisers, seafoods in crystal goblets, a selection of delectable cold meats and a variety of salads. Flans piled high with fruit were decorated with whipped cream and topped with slices of a silvery-green fruit that was unfamiliar to her. There were flat dishes piled with crisp snowy mounds, lashings of whipped cream, and strewn with pinkish-green seeds.

Nicola turned to the youth at her side, indicating one of the snowy concoctions. 'Could that be what they call a Pavlova?' she whispered.

He seemed to find his tongue at last. 'That's right. It's known as the national dessert—why don't you try some?' Before she could protest he had cut a gigantic slice of the marshmallow sweet and piled it on to her plate. 'You'll like the passionfruit topping too.'

She stared back at him incredulously. 'Did you say *passion*fruit?' The next moment she regretted having pursued the subject, for it was evident that her young companion was once again overcome with shyness. To change the subject she glanced around the crowded table, and commented, 'Sharon isn't here?'

In a sudden lull in the buzz of conversation, the words were clearly audible, and it was Mrs Hazlett who answered.

'Yes, where is Sharon? John,' she called across the table to her son, 'do you know what's happened to her? She's not ill, is she?'

He said in a muffled tone, 'She said to tell you she's not hungry.' His laugh had a forced note. 'All those goodies this afternoon must have been a bit too much for her to take.'

An older woman seated at his side nodded sagely. 'Probably she's slimming. All the girls are nowadays.'

'Slimming!' John's father put in. 'She's the slimmest girl I ever saw in my life. Any slimmer and she wouldn't be there at all. All a lot of nonsense! Go along and fetch her, John.'

John stared down at his plate. 'It's no use, Dad. Once Sharon's made up her mind that's it.'

The older man sent him a thoughtful glance. 'Taking Sharon to the ball tonight, aren't you?'

'Of course. That's the whole idea of her coming to stay for the weekend.'

'That's all right, then.'

When the meal was over Nicola delayed returning to the room she shared with Sharon for as long as possible. In the spacious lounge with a crowd of strangers she was content to sit quietly and let the tide of laughter and chatter and reminiscences of old goldmining days flow around her. When at last she reached the bedroom she found the room in darkness. A muffled sob came from a twin bed by the wall. 'Don't put on the light.'

Nicola said gently, 'Is there anything I can do?'

'Go away and leave me alone, that's what!'

Suddenly a light flashed on, revealing the other girl's tear-blotched face and rumpled hair. John stood in the doorway. 'Come on, Sharon.' He hesitated. 'You are coming with me, aren't you?'

'How many times do I have to tell you!' she flung at him. 'No, no, no!'

He crossed the room to seat himself beside her, smoothing back the tumbled hair from her forehead. 'You shouldn't get all uptight about Mother. If only you wouldn't argue with her! It's not good for her state of health. You've upset her——'

'I've upset her? I like that! It's she who——'

'She's only thinking of you, trying to help you.'

'She's got a funny way of going about it, then. Telling me I shouldn't smoke cigarettes, saying my dresses are cut too low. As if,' she cried with feeling, 'it's anything to do with her!' The low tones were fraught with emotion. 'I'm sick and tired of her interfering with everything I do, and if you cared, if you really cared about me——'

As Nicola slipped from the room, the angry voices followed her. 'No, I'm not going to your beastly ball! What if you have made all the arrangements? I can't get it through to you, can I? I just don't care! Why don't you take her, the English girl, if you're so determined on going.'

'I might at that.'

'Go on, then! I don't care who you take!'

Nicola slipped back to her seat in a shadowy corner of the big lounge. She was still there half an hour later when the youth whom she had met at dinner came to seek her out.

'John says to tell you he's just had a phone call telling him there are a couple of cancellations for the centenary ball tonight. I mean,' all at once he was self-conscious, glancing down at his big hands, 'if you'd care to come along, we could all go, you and me and John and Sharon.'

'Sharon?' Nicola was surprised. 'She's going, then?'

'Oh yes, she's coming. I was speaking to her just now and she's just about ready. Would you,' a dull tide of red crept up the boyish face, 'would you come as my partner?'

She smiled up into the eager young face. 'Why not?' Something in his expression, a mixture of hope and longing and shyness, told her that the invitation meant a lot to him. A teasing smile curved her lips. 'It's your first ball, is that it?'

He nodded, his face serious. 'If you'll come with me. It all depends on you, Miss Ayres.'

'I'll come—I never did catch your name.'

'It's Bruce.' An expression of sheer happiness flooded his face. 'Gee, that's mighty!' He added shyly, 'You're Nicola, aren't you?'

'That's me!' She got to her feet. 'Give me ten minutes, Bruce, and I'll be ready!'

CHAPTER TWO

'Now that's an idea.' Mrs Hazlett had overheard the diffident boyish tones. 'It will be an experience for you, Nicola. I suppose you've got something to wear?'

Nicola nodded. 'It's not exactly a ball gown, but it will have to do.'

Nicola felt rather reluctant to return to the same room as Sharon when the other girl was clearly distressed and strung up, no doubt because of her quarrel with John. When she opened the door, however, she found to her relief that the room was empty and only the low murmur of voices from the porch leading off the french doors told her that Sharon and John were continuing their argument out there in the darkness.

Swiftly Nicola changed into a long slinky cream-coloured dress with narrow shoulder straps. She touched her mouth with lipstick once again and slipped her feet into light-coloured shoes with slender high heels. There, that should complete her preparations. She smiled, humming a tune to herself. Not that her boyish escort would be all that critical of her appearance. Painfully self-conscious and nervous of taking a partner to his first ball as he was, she suspected that all his thoughts would be centred on himself.

She could hear the sound of voices from the porch as she let herself out of the room and went into the lounge. Immediately she was greeted by a chorus of feminine compliments and masculine whistles of appreciation. Much more of this, she told herself, and it would be going to her head—the novelty of the strange environment, the delightful warmth of the air, the admiring glances from all these strangers. All at once she caught sight of her reflection in a long mirror on the wall. That couldn't be herself, that radiant-looking girl! What had happened to her? She became aware that Bruce had come to join her. Looking ill at ease in his dinner jacket, hair slicked down on a sunburned forehead, he had a shy admiring glance for her. 'Gee, you look terrific!'

She laughed. 'Think so? How about yourself?'

He gazed selfconsciously downwards. 'The legs of this suit are a bit short. It's an old one of John's that I borrowed for the night. The sleeves too,' he tugged at the wrist of his jacket, 'but if you don't mind——'

'No one will ever notice,' she assured him.

'Gee,' his eyes were shining with sudden happiness, 'I'm

glad you came along tonight.'

She laughed and tucked her arm in his. 'Me too!'

'You look lovely, my dear.' Mrs Hazlett had come to stand beside her. 'That outfit you're wearing is quite lovely, but it could do with just one little touch—wait a moment and I'll show you what I mean!' She hurried out of the room, to return almost at once, a lacy black shawl draped over her arm. 'This is the shawl I wore to my very first ball in the same hall where you're going tonight, and the shawl was years and years old then. Wouldn't it be nice, don't you think, if you were to wear it tonight? After all,' she gave her thin smile, 'it is a centenary ball. There!' Before Nicola could make an answer the older woman had draped the garment around her shoulders. 'Let me fasten it for you with this!' She pinned the ends of the shawl together with a black silk rose. 'Now,' she stood back to admire the effect, then glanced around the room, 'what do you think? Isn't that an improvement? It isn't every girl who has a chance of wearing a shawl that's over a hundred years old!'

'Is it really as old as that?' What would she feel like, she wondered apprehensively, if she were to damage the fragile threads? She made a mental note to shed the heirloom just as soon as she found an opportunity.

The next moment she became aware of Sharon. The other girl was standing not far away and although the skilful application of make-up had disguised her swollen eyelids, there was no mistaking the other girl's resentful expression. Here was one person, Nicola reflected, who didn't take kindly to her hostess's suggestion.

It was clear that Mrs Hazlett too had caught Sharon's tight-lipped glance. 'Don't take any notice of Sharon,' she told Nicola in her brisk way, 'she's only sorry she didn't take the chance of wearing the shawl herself when I offered it to her tonight.'

'*Sorry!*' Sharon choked on the word and John said in his measured accents,

'Come along, Shar, we'd better get going—coming Bruce?'

A chorus of 'Goodnight' and 'Have a good time' echoed around them as they left the room. Soon they were piling into a late model car standing in the wide driveway, and to Nicola it seemed no time at all before they were moving up the main street of the town and John was pulling up amongst a line of cars, trucks and Land Rovers standing outside a brightly lit building.

As they made their way inside the hall, John and Sharon, who appeared to know everyone in sight, stopped to chat, and Nicola soon lost count of the young people to whom she had been introduced. Then at last they were seated at a table and John ordered drinks. Nicola, glancing around her, took in banners hanging from strings from the ceiling of the old building, stylised scenes of old goldmining days in the district. In the crowd she caught glimpses of men attired in old-time three-piece suits with stiffened, stand-up collars. A group of girls drifted by in graceful period dresses—probably, Nicola mused, gowns that had been kept in their families for generations. And that reminded her—she began to unfasten the shawl around her shoulders.

One man stood out in the crowd, at least he did to her. So tall and upstanding and so very ... attractive. She went on watching him threading his way, or rather, determinedly pushing his way—she could scarcely believe her luck—in the direction of their table. Fearful that he might catch the look of interest in her eyes, she glanced away, to hear John's even tones.

'Nicola—Keith. He's one of our party tonight.'

'So we meet again.'

That cultured voice, that *well-remembered* voice! She glanced up to meet the mocking gaze of a man who was vaguely familiar.

'That's right, we've met before.' He was regarding her with wickedly merry eyes.

Nicola opened her lips, then closed them again. It couldn't be, and yet—— 'It was *you*!' Shock and bewilderment made the words burst incredulously from her lips.

'You were driving a truck for the Lorimer Timber Company——'

'Driving for them?' Sharon's jeering laughter broke across her words. 'Keith *is* the Lorimer Timber Company.'

'Oh!' At the amused glint in his eyes, Nicola wished herself a hundred miles away.

'We got acquainted on the road today,' he told the other two. 'Has Miss Ayres let you into her reason for coming out to this part of the world?'

For a moment John's heavy glance lightened. 'There hasn't been much time, with the crowd at home and all that. We've scarcely had a word with her.'

Sharon's eyes sparkled with malice. 'Don't tell me! Let me guess! How about husband-hunting, fresh fields?'

Nicola was beginning to recover her composure. She decided to ignore Sharon's sarcastic remarks. After all, the girl did have problems of her own this evening. No wonder she was lashing out at anyone who happened to be handy! Aloud she said, 'No, it's not a husband that I'm looking for, not even a boy-friend. It happens to be an uncle. I'm trying to trace him. His name is Walter Fletcher and he'd be getting on in years now. Does the name ring a bell? No? Oh well, I guess that would have made it all just too easy.'

John said curiously, 'Did he live in the district?'

She shrugged. 'I wish I knew. All I know for sure is that he was last heard of in Waihi. He could have found work in the goldmine here, but that was ages ago, so I expect I'm in for a search even to find any record of him. It's because of my aunt really. She's a dear, she's been awfully good to me. She even paid for my trip out here. All I have to do in return is to try and find out what's happened to her only brother.'

Keith Lorimer raised his glass, his mocking glance holding hers. 'Here's luck with your search!'

At that moment the musicians seated on the stage broke into a foot-tapping rhythm and that distracting, hateful, smiling man had risen to her feet and was bending attentively towards her. 'Dance?' What could she do but let him guide her towards the dance floor and avoid his gaze as they followed the beat of the latest pop melody?

When at last they retraced their steps to the table she remembered to her mortification that Keith Lorimer was one of the party. Over drinks she turned to talk to Bruce, yet she found her ears alerted to the conversation going on across the table.

'What happened to your partner?' John was saying. 'Annabel seemed keen to make up a party for tonight when she rang me last week about the tickets.'

Annabel. Who was Annabel, Nicola wondered, and why was she so interested in a strange girl anyway?

'Oh, she was, she was, but you know Annabel.' Keith didn't seem overly disappointed at the non-appearance of the unknown girl. 'She was all ready to come back to the house this week when there was a hitch in some dress she's working on for the Gown of the Year Contest, so she decided to stay in town and concentrate on her entry.'

John nodded. 'Sounds like Annabel. A perfectionist if ever there was one! Think she'll have a chance of raking in the prize?'

Keith's smile seemed to Nicola to radiate utter confidence. 'You know Annabel. Winning the award will really put her on her way!'

The trick was, she told herself, to avoid meeting Keith's mocking glance. Almost she felt as though she were drowning in those dark depths, while he watched her, amused at the unfamiliar emotions she was trying so hard to conceal. The music had started up once again and she left the table with Bruce. Almost it was a relief to escape Keith's nearness. It must surely be her own sense of mortification that made her so *aware* of him, for never before had she felt this way about any man.

Bruce's self-conscious feelings made his movements stiff and unresponsive, all his energies directed on his dance steps, but gradually as the evening wore on he lost his awkwardness and, flushed and excited, forgot his feet and enjoyed moving with the rhythm of the melody.

As to Nicola, she was only too pleased to have Bruce

as her partner. Not only did his company rescue her from
the necessity of making small talk with Keith Lorimer—
her cheeks burned at the thought of the way in which she
had treated him, the mistaken way she had regarded him—
but she was glad to escape from the strained atmosphere
that prevailed between John and Sharon. She suspected
that the other girl's flushed cheeks were due to anger and
resentment and John, silent and unresponsive, showed
no evidence of enjoying the evening.

It was an hour or two later when the men had gone to
fetch drinks that Nicola found herself alone at the table
with Sharon.

'You're not wearing your shawl,' Sharon said, 'is it too
hot?'

Once again Nicola decided to ignore the antagonistic
note in the low, taut accents. 'I've no idea whether it's hot
or not, and I'm not risking wearing it to find out. I mean,
one hundred years old, and so fine and cobwebby and
sort of frail. If anything happened to it after all that time
and I was the one who ruined it——'

'I'd be glad,' Sharon said fiercely, 'if it fell to bits.'

'Glad?'

'Sure I would! John's mother has ruined my evening.'
Her voice was low and husky with emotion. 'She wanted me
to wear her stupid old shawl. She went on and on about
it and then John took her part—he always does. Something seemed to snap in me,' she crushed out her cigar-
ette in the ashtray with stabbing movements, 'and I just
blew up. All of a sudden I couldn't stand it any longer, the
way he's always on her side when she interferes between us
and there's trouble like there was tonight.' Nicola's silence
seemed to break down the barriers of reserve and the words
came in a flood. 'She thinks she can order me about, tell
me what to do. Just because she once wore the stupid
old shawl to a ball she decided I had to do the same! She
just takes over! The trouble is,' Nicola barely caught the
low murmur, 'he's *her* son and she'll never let him go!
She means to part us, anyone can see what she's up to—
anyone but John, that is. He's such a *fool* where she's con-

cerned.' She seemed to be speaking to herself, twisting her empty glass from side to side. 'He's her only son. There was another boy, a bit older, but he was killed some years ago in a motorbike accident. Now she thinks the sun, moon and stars shine out of John and she's determined that no girl is going to take him from her. Oh, she'd never admit that she feels that way. According to her, she's always just trying to help me.' Sharon seemed to be staring at Nicola without really seeing her. 'There was another girl he cared about once. They were engaged to be married and the wedding date was set, then suddenly everything was off.' She snapped her fingers in the air. 'Just like that! And I bet it was *her* doing! If only,' she sighed in a distraught tone, 'John could see what his mother is trying to do to us, but he never will.'

So John's mother was the cause of the rift between them, Nicola thought, but the men had returned to the table and she couldn't think about anyone else's problems, not with Keith Lorimer seated close at her side, too close for her peace of mind. Presently John and Sharon moved towards the dance floor and Bruce, more confident now of his dancing abilities, went to seek another partner. Left alone with Keith, Nicola was aware of a discomfiting silence, at least that was the way it seemed to her. She would have to say *something* to him, not a straight-out apology, she simply couldn't humble herself to do that, but—— The words that fell from her lips were quite different from the smooth and careless remark she had planned, an accusing, 'You might have told me!'

The dark thick brows rose enquiringly. 'Told you what?' His tone was deceptively casual.

'Oh, you know!' Even to her own ears her voice sounded like that of a petulant child. 'About who you were!'

He said softly, 'Would it have made any difference?'

Now she felt more abashed than ever, a prig and a snob as well as everything else.

'Well,' she cried hotly, 'it was your own fault! I don't usually take rides with rough-and-tough timber workers.' His amused glance made her more than ever uneasy. 'It

was those clothes you were wearing, That awful hat! Did
you have to wear it?'

He put on a hurt expression. 'How can you talk like
that? That hat is unique, the only one of its kind in the
country, I'd say——'

'Thank heaven for that!'

He ignored her comment. 'I'll have you know that I had
the devil's own job to get hold of it. Took me a week of
searching to run it to earth.'

She stared at him incredulously. 'I don't believe it!'

He gave a shout of laughter that made a couple at the
adjoining table turn to eye them curiously. 'You just don't
know, do you?'

Was he laughing at her? 'No, I don't,' she said crossly,
'and you never bother to explain all the mystery.'

Amusement lingered in the dark eyes that rested on her
face. 'Right, I'll let you in on it. It was all part of a re-
enactment scene got up by the local organisers of the
centenary week celebrations. I'll have you know, Miss
Ayres, that you see before you a direct descendant of the
first man to put his pick in the hillside and discover gold
and silver right there on Martha Hill.'

She didn't know what to say. 'Really?'

He picked up his glass. 'So, me being the one who was
in the picture, they asked me to do the big re-enactment
scene up on the hill where it all happened. Actually, it
wasn't exactly the same as the original happening,' went on
the deep voice with a chuckle. 'Oh, I did my bit all
right, swung the pick into the hillside and all that——'

She didn't know whether her anger was with herself for
being such a stupid idiot as to have been taken in by his
scruffy appearance or towards him because of the huge
enjoyment he seemed to be getting at her mortification.
'What did you say at the big moment?' she enquired
coldly, 'Look at me, everyone! I've found the hidden
treasure! Hallelujah!'

It was useless. Her sarcasm was wasted on him. He was
grinning, showing those white teeth against the deep tan.
She was glad now that she hadn't glimpsed his eyes during

their drive together. They were altogether too ... exciting.
They held her with a bright alive fire in their depths so
that she couldn't sustain his look. With an effort she
wrenched her mind back to the vibrant tones.

'Something like that. What I didn't have to worry about
today was all the trouble my great-grandfather struck on
his big day.'

'What short of trouble?' She found herself interested in
spite of herself.

'Well, it seems that by bad luck the site where the gold
was first found happened to be the site of a Maori burial
ground and angry Maoris tried to stop the digging in land
that was *tapu*——'

'*Tapu?*'

'Sacred to the Maoris,' he explained, serious now. 'Not
to be touched or disturbed—ever. Anyway, it seems the
local Maoris decided to stop the digging in *tapu* land by
bringing along their heaviest and largest women to scare
off the prospectors. The women did their bit by screaming
non-stop and in the end drove the prospectors to under-
ground mining.'

She eyed him suspiciously. 'You're having me on!'

Once again he was wearing his bland expression. 'How
can you say that, Miss Ayres? Would I do such a thing?'

'You did this afternoon,' she reminded him huffily.

'Just because you happened to get the wrong idea——'

She realised she was getting out of her depth and hurried
to bring the conversation back to safer channels. 'So you
were on the way back from the re-enactment scene when
you picked me up?'

'That's right. I got a bit held up on the hill, a spot of
celebrating, you understand? It was fairly late when I
climbed into the truck to come back.'

'Wasn't I lucky?' Could that be her own voice, so cool
and cutting (or trying to be)? The annoying thing about
the man was that you couldn't seem to rattle that amused
composure of his. She became aware of his thoughtful
gaze.

'Got any big plans for your detective work?'

She shook her head, murmured, 'Not yet,' and the next moment realised that she had played right into his hands. 'I could take you around a few of the local places. You never know your luck, you might pick up some information at the local museum. It's a good time to see around with all the centennial stuff on display. There's a concert on at the end of the week, you simply can't afford to miss that.' Was he having a joke at her expense? She couldn't tell. 'All the old-time miners will turn up that night. I'll be the only male in the place who's under sixty, but I'll put up with it,' she caught his teasing grin, 'for you—and Uncle Walter!'

'I'm sorry,' she sought wildly in her mind for an excuse, 'I can't say what I'll be doing in the next few days. The Hazletts——'

'That's all right, you go along with Keith, Nicola.' To her chagrin John had come back to the table and had overheard the last few words. 'You'll enjoy having a look around the place,' he added in his measured tones.

Enjoy going *anywhere* with Keith Lorimer as guide and companion! At that moment she chanced to catch Bruce's wistful glance. 'Tomorrow I promised to take a local tour with Bruce,' she said. In the turmoil of her thoughts she was struck by the way the boyish face had lit up.

'That's right,' Bruce followed her lead.

'Okay,' the Lorimer man appeared quite unperturbed by her obvious reluctance to accept his invitation, 'just as you like!'

Perversely, now that she had tossed away the opportunity he had offered her, she found herself longing for that very thing. Not that she liked the man—on the contrary. Just because there was something about him that affected her oddly, drew sparks in her, it didn't follow that she was drawn to his particular brand of dark good looks. But he knew the town and the folk who lived here and he might have been able to help her, far more than young Bruce, in her search for Uncle Walter. *Liar.* A voice spoke in her mind. He attracts you and you know it. She pushed aside the niggle of truth. All the more reason not to see any more of him.

When she awoke in the morning the feeling of vague regret was still with her. Ridiculous, really. She wouldn't let herself dwell on the day she might have spent with that maddening Keith Lorimer. After all, she would be here for eight weeks and anything could happen—she brought her thoughts up short. There she went again, dwelling on him.

She was wearing jeans today, a snowy T-shirt, blue sneakers. Her hair tied back from her ears with a ribbon, and feeling fresh and ready for the day, she went in to breakfast. The meal, she found, was a casual one, with guests free to get up when they pleased and help themselves to cornflakes, milk, tea and coffee. She had left Sharon apparently still asleep in bed and there was no sign of John or his father.

'Morning, Nicola. Did you enjoy the ball last night?' Mrs Hazlett bustled towards her and slipped a piece of bread into the toaster. 'Dad and I have scarcely had a chance to speak to you yet,' she threw over her shoulder, 'and Bruce tells me that he's showing you around the town today. Dad is lending him the car.' Before she could make a reply the chatty tones flowed on. 'John has been telling me about how you're out in this part of the world to try to trace your uncle. I've done a bit of study on genealogy myself and I'll jot down a few notes for you to follow. It's quite important to know where to start. But John will help you.' All at once her face glowed with motherly pride. 'Being a fully qualified lawyer, he'll be able to give you lots of helpful advice. He's always so good about helping people. Just ask him anything you want to know.'

'I really don't think——'

Mrs Hazlett took not the slightest notice of Nicola's protest. 'It won't do you any harm though to see around the town today and get an idea of the place, then once you have my notes you'll be able to get going with your enquiries.' Nicola was beginning to understand Sharon's reference to John's mother 'taking over'. 'Here comes Bruce now!'

His face scrubbed and shining and hair brushed over his forehead, Bruce came hurrying towards Nicola. She noticed the anxious expression in his eyes. 'You're still coming out with me today?'

'Did you think,' she said teasingly, 'that I'd have changed my mind since last night?' At his obvious embarrassment she added laughingly, 'Don't worry, I can hardly wait. When do we set off?'

'As soon as you like!' The eager tones betrayed his inner excitement. 'You don't mind if we take Ben—John's dog— along?'

'Of course not,' she smiled.

A short time later they were driving along a quiet street and approaching the shopping centre of the town, John's Corgi sitting quietly on the back sea. 'Let's have a walk up the main street,' Nicola suggested, 'I can see more that way.'

'If you like.' Clearly Bruce was intoxicated with the late model car and would have liked nothing better than to spend the day at the wheel. He parked the vehicle good-naturedly enough, however, and they strolled up the main thoroughfare, pausing to study specimens of gold-bearing quartz and old models of machinery that were on display in the stores.

Back in the car, they moved along quiet suburban streets with their gaily painted timber houses surrounded by spacious lawns and bright with flowering trees and shrubs. Then all at once they came in sight of a small lake where native bush crowded down to the waters edge and swans and wild duck moved on a wind-ruffled surface. They got out of the car to stand at the edge of the lake, behind them a backdrop of a bush-covered hill, dark away from the sun. 'When the supply of gold in the hill ran out at last,' Bruce told her, 'they flooded the mine and made this lake.' Moving over a small white bridge spanning lake water, they took a path winding ahead amongst tall native trees. It was as they emerged into the sunlight of a clearing that

Nicola caught sight of crumbling stone ruins rising sheer from encroaching bush and creepers and scrub. 'What on earth——'

'It's all that's left of the old pump house on Martha Hill.' Bruce followed her gaze towards the high stone wall reaching for the sky.

'My goodness!' Nicola was still staring at empty arch-ways. 'It looks like the ruins of an old castle. Let's go and take a closer look!'

Together they took a narrow path leading up the hill-side, and soon they were scrambling up through thickly growing bush and fern towards the grey walls above. As they came nearer to the deserted old pump house Nicola realised that the earth on which it stood had crumbled away to high cliffs, overgrown with creepers and bushes, where a false step could send one tumbling down the de-ceptive cliff face. On these slopes, though, there seemed no danger and while she and Bruce made their way towards the ruined pump house on the summit of the hill, the corgi frisked around them.

At last they reached the top of the hill, making their way carefully around the crumbling cliff edge towards an open-ing in the stone wall, Nicola glanced down the shaft of the dark interior, then raised her eyes to the wall rising high above. Vaguely she was aware of groups of sightseers milling around her. Of course, the town would be full of visitors this week. For a moment her attention was caught by a man who was partially obscured by the party he was with. There was something familiar about that straight back. The next moment the corgi dashed past her. Intent on some purpose of his own, the dog was making straight for the crumbling cliff edge with its warning sign, DANGER.

'Ben! Come back!' Her warning scream rang out as she ran in pursuit, only to see the dog vanish over the edge. She could see him struggling and terrified, as he fought to make his way from the creepers that halted his fall. He wasn't very far below. She dropped to her knees and peered over the edge. She could reach him from here ... almost.

Vaguely she was aware of people calling, of Bruce's frenzied shout, 'Don't move. I'll get him!' But Ben, almost free of the entanglement, was beginning to slide downwards and if she didn't grab him now, this minute, it would be too late. She made a frantic effort to reach the panicky animal, overbalanced, and the next moment she was tumbling over and over in a shower of rubble, choking and gasping ... That was the last thing she remembered, the sensation of falling, of trying to grasp at nothing. Then there was only a swirling of colours, red, black, faster, faster, then total blackness, oblivion.

She came back to her senses slowly. For a while she couldn't make out where she was. She lay blinking, staring out of a window that framed a view of pine trees, rows and rows of them, all in formation. Pine trees? No help there in trying to decide where she was. Her gaze wandered around the room, a big room with a high, old-fashioned ceiling and heavy furniture, faded rugs on a polished floor. Another mystery was her suitcase, thrown on the cream candlewick bedspread of the other twin bed. It was all very strange, but there was nothing unreal about the throbbing of her head. Gingerly she put up a hand to the back of her head and touched a painful swelling. She realised she was now dressed in pyjamas. So that meant—slowly her sluggish mind came up with the answer—there must have been an accident. An accident at the old pump house! All at once it all came rushing back—Ben disappearing over the cliff edge, her efforts to save him.

A tap at the door interrupted her musing and she called, 'Come in.'

The next moment she wondered if she would have done that had she known that it would be Keith Lorimer who would come strolling into the room towards her. Oddly, the dark eyes had lost their teasing sparkle and were deep with some other emotion that was almost like—relief? But how could that be?

His words were ordinary enough. 'Feeling all right?'

She fingered the swelling on the back of her head. 'Ye-es,

I guess so. I just can't understand——' Suddenly a light seemed to flash on in her mind. 'This is *your* home!' Funny how she had forgotten so many things today, but the name stayed with her. 'This is Sky Lodge!'

'Right.' He dropped down to the bed.

'But I still don't know how I come to be here——'

'You're here because I brought you.' He put up a hand to smooth back the dark strands of hair falling across her forehead. 'You took a header over the cliff at the old pump house on the hill, remember?'

Her eyes widened. 'Ben—the dog—is he all right?'

'He's okay. A lot better than you are, actually. Not that the little devil deserves to be, getting you into all this. He was stuck on a ledge half way down the cliff, barking his head off, when I got to him, but I left him where he was until I'd seen to you.'

She digested the information in silence. Then, 'You did that? Rescued me? You didn't have to drag me right back to the top? How can I ever——'

He disclaimed her thanks. 'It was nothing. I've done plenty of rock climbing all over the country and it was just that I happened to be on the spot before anyone else. I don't mind telling you it gave me one hell of a fright seeing you lying there at the foot of the cliff. It really threw me, not knowing how badly hurt you were.'

'All the same——'

Once again he waved away her attempt to thank him. 'So then I ran you to hospital and the doctors made certain there was no serious damage, just a spot of concussion. A day or two's rest is all you need, they said, and you'll be as good as new.'

'Concussion?' she echoed, and thought, So that is why it's almost dark outside. Somehow I've missed out on most of the day. She brought her mind back to the deep, vibrant tones.

'So then I brought you up here.'

Could it be the cliff tumble that was making her so stupidly slow in the uptake. 'But why did you do that?'

'Why here, you mean? Doctor's orders, that's the answer

to that one.' Nicola had learned to distrust the wicked
light that gleamed in the depths of his dark eyes. 'When it
came to the point I had no choice in the matter. Rest,
they told me, quiet, they said, that's all she needs now,
and with the crowd at Hazletts' place ... Bet you have to
share a room down there?'

'Well, yes, but ...' Was she imagining the glint in his
eyes, a gleam of amusement that could mean anything,
like, 'I wanted it this way, that's why!' Trouble was that
she was feeling too foggy-minded to follow the problem
to its logical conclusion.

'So I sent young Bruce back to Hazletts to let them in on
what was happening. Seems they're quite happy about the
arrangement. They agreed that I'd done the right thing
in bringing you here. Now relax, Miss Ayres. If you're
wondering if I'm here on my own, I've got a housekeeper.
Molly's a friend of the family who likes nothing better
than to fuss around visitors. So,' he was wearing his
amused look once again, 'what are you worrying about?'

What *was* she worrying about? She wrenched her mind
back to his voice. 'Take it easy and rest up for a day or
so. That's all you have to do.'

She was still trying to piece things together. 'What time
is it?' she asked bewilderedly.

'You mean, what day is it? You were out to the world
all day yesterday and now it's nine o'clock on a brand
new day—how do you feel?'

She moved uncomfortably. 'A bit sore.'

'Bruises. They'll wear off. Know something?' His voice
deepened to a serious note. 'You were lucky to come out
of that cliff fall alive!'

'Thanks to you.' All at once realisation swept her.
Supposing she had hit her head on the rock face as she
crashed through the bushes? Supposing she hadn't been
rescued so quickly and rushed to a doctor for treatment?'
She said very low, 'You could say that you ... really ...
saved my life?'

Keith grinned his heart-warming smile. 'I just happened

to be the one who was handy at the right moment. My lucky day!'

She couldn't quite meet his dancing glance. A tap at the door saved her from making an answer, even had she been able to think up a suitable reply. The next moment a big woman with an open face and untidy blonde hair was regarding her with a friendly smile. 'I'm Molly, and I know you're Miss Ayres. You're awake, then? Thank heaven for that! All day yesterday I thought you were never going to come to.' So this kindly woman had been keeping watch at her bedside for hours, Nicola thought in surprise. 'Keith and I were real worried about you. You'll be ready for a cuppa now, I'll be bound, and a nice bit of toast to go with it. I'll bring you in a tray in a couple of minutes.'

'Thank you, I'd like that.'

'I'm off now,' Keith was saying. Nicola intercepted the significant glance he flashed towards the housekeeper. 'You'll let me know right away if you need me? I'll be working down at the mill, so give me a ring if you're in any doubt at all and I'll be right back.'

Molly nodded understandingly. 'Don't worry, I'll take good care of her.'

'Right!' He paused in the doorway, a tall sinewy-looking man in lived-in cord slacks, a crimson work shirt and a look in his eyes that made her feel all at once cherished and cared for. She felf a wild sweet tide of happiness surge through her. The warm feeling stayed with her all the time she dealt with the light breakfast Molly had brought her.

When the housekeeper came back to the room Nicola was lying back on the pillows, dark hair fanning out around her shoulders.

'Tell me something Molly. Keith owns this place? Sky Lodge, that's the name, isn't it?'

'That's right.' Molly crossed the room to pull aside the curtains and fling open the windows, and Nicola glanced out towards the long symmetrical rows of sombre that clothed the hillside. 'His grandfather built the house,' Molly went on, 'it was a farmhouse in those days and in Keith's father's time too. But Keith was always a timber man and when he took over the property he planted the hill in pines and built a sawmill down on the flat.' She added irrelevantly, 'He'll *kill* me if I don't keep you in bed all day!'

'Never mind about that. How long have you been working for him, Molly?'

'Oh, for ages and ages. Ever since my husband died, ten years ago.'

Nicola hadn't meant to sound gossipy and nosey, but somehow the words slipped out. 'You would have thought, wouldn't you, that he would be married by now, a man like that?'

Molly showed no surprise at the question. Maybe, Nicola thought, the housekeeper had had the same query put to her many times before.

She said slowly, 'He would have been married five years ago, if Janice hadn't died.'

Nicola echoed quickly, 'Died?'

Molly nodded. 'Janice was a nurse at the hospital and driving home late one night, her car was involved in a head-on smash. She was killed instantly. It was too bad when she and Keith were all set to be married in a month's time. Oh well, it's all a long time ago now and these things happen. How about you, love? You've come out here for the centenary celebrations, I expect, like all the other visitors in town this fortnight?'

'Something like that.' Nicola spoke absently, her mind still on Keith. The sneaky thought kept creeping in that she was glad he was free, glad that he *seemed* to like her. Almost it was worth suffering the fall over the cliff to find herself right here at Sky Lodge, *with him*!

CHAPTER THREE

TIME passed. Nicola, dozing and dreaming, was content to let the hours slide by. Once she dreamed that Keith was kissing her and she awoke with startled eyes to find him standing at her bedside, close, but not *that* close! Because of the vividness of the dream she felt selfconscious just looking at him, and made a pretence of still feeling hazy until he bent over her solicitously.

'You awake Nicola?' *Nicola*. She was glad she had stopped being Miss Ayres to him.

'I guess I'm still feeling a bit dopey.'

'You won't want to be bothered with visitors, then. The Hazletts are clamouring at the door, but if you don't feel up to seeing them I'll tell them to come back tomorrow.'

She raised herself on an elbow. 'No, no, I'm all right.' She could scarcely explain to him that it wasn't the Hazlett family who were on her mind at the moment.

She could scarcely suppress a smile as the group tiptoed into the room. In the end she burst out laughing. 'I'm not sick, you know!'

'You'd better tell that to young Bruce,' John's father told her, 'he's going around the place looking as though he's responsible for having pushed you over the cliff.'

The words did nothing to lighten the unhappy expression on the boyish face. 'Gee, I'm sorry, Nicola,' Bruce mumbled. 'If only I'd been looking——'

'It wouldn't have made any difference,' she assured him lightly. 'You just weren't close enough to warn me not to be so stupid.'

He looked a little happier. 'You couldn't have known the ground would crumble away under your feet.'

She said teasingly, 'With all those notices around the place, saying "Danger, Keep Out"! I just ignored them, that was all.'

'If we can do anything for you—' Mrs Hazlett's bright gaze went to Nicola's glowing face. 'You look all right... Keith says you're to stay here for the rest of the week, but there's really no need, your room at home is free now.' Nicola caught the triumphant note in the feminine tones, and glancing towards John, took in the look of strain around his mouth. Mrs Hazlett answered Nicola's unspoken query. 'John is free too, now that he and Sharon have—'

'You're sure there's nothing we can get you?' John broke in in his measured tones. 'This is just something to go on with— some fruits, magazines.' He laid on the bedside table a pile of women's magazines and a basket of apples, mandarins and early peaches. 'We'll try to make it up to you. Come back tomorrow if you can.'

They were all being so hospitable that Nicola felt a twinge of compunction, for somehow she didn't want to leave Sky Lodge, not just yet. Sky Lodge—or the owner? She shied away from the answer to the query.

She twinkled up at John. 'If you really want to help, and you're not too busy in the office, how about giving me some professional advice as to how to go about tracing my missing relative?'

For a moment his grim expression relaxed. 'Can do. I've got access to volumes of the old electoral rolls. His name should be included there if he once lived in the district.'

'That would be a wonderful help.'

'I'm not promising anything. Not everyone's name was included in the rolls in those days, but there are other avenues I'll follow up. Things like land and estate records, deeds and titles, mortgages, wills, tax records, account books, to name a few.'

Nicola looked across at him in amazement. 'I never thought of things alike that.'

He shrugged. 'Oh, it isn't the first genealogy thing I've had to follow up. There all sorts of other ways to glean information.'

'You don't need to worry about finding your uncle.'

Mrs Hazlett was regarding her son with open admiration and it was clear that to her the quest was as good as over already. No wonder, Nicola mused, that Sharon didn't fit into the close family circle. Didn't fit, or wasn't wanted? She brought her mind back to the feminine tones. 'Anyway, John, it will give you something to think about just now, take your mind off Sharon.'

He didn't answer, and shortly afterwards the party moved away and Nicola heard Keith's voice as he escorted them to the waiting car.

Nicola lay thinking about John. She was lucky in having such expert help with her search. It was clear that the engagement had been broken off and judging by the defeated expression in John's face, he was taking the break badly. Probably Sharon was too. Kind though Mrs Hazlett was to her, kind but managing, Nicola couldn't help the thought that John's mother had had a lot to do with the broken engagement—the second engagement to which she had put an end, according to what Sharon had told her. If only John weren't so quiet and repressed, and so much concerned with his mother's state of health.

It was later in the afternoon when she realised she was feeling perfectly well and that lying here was just a waste of time. Taking a floral brunch coat from her suitcase, she picked up a fluffy towel Molly had left on the rail, and tiptoed out of the room and down the deserted hall. Maybe if Keith saw for himself how well she was now he might have some ideas of inviting her outside to look around his property. She would just *have* to look healthy!

She soon found, however, that she had no need to pretend to good health, for back in her room after a warm shower, wearing fresh undies and bra and a cool dress of misty blue, she could find nothing amiss with her appearance. There were scratches on her face and arms that make-up had covered, and odd bruises on her body, but these didn't worry her. On the contrary, she reflected, for some odd reason she looked positively radiant. The clear New Zealand air must be doing something for her.

That reminds me, she thought, I must ask Keith to look

up those old newspapers and records he told me he had here. Keith ... her eyes were dreamy. She couldn't seem to get him out of her mind. A guilty conscience probably, because of the way she had acted towards him when he had picked her up in his timber truck. He seemed to strike sparks of anger in her, sparks which he apparently delighted in arousing, and yet somehow she found him interesting—very.

Moving to the window, she leaned from the opening and gazed at the vista spread around her. From here on a hill—a mountain she would have called it at home— the road curved to meet the highway below, and the town she had left looked far away. From up here, almost in the clouds, she saw that the long drive to the house was cut between plantations of pine trees with their long fire-breaks. On the flat below she made out the outlines of a timber mill.

At that moment a Land Rover came into sight around a curve of the long driveway. Nicola watched as it came nearer, to draw up at the entrance. Keith dropped down from the vehicle, then looking up to catch sight of her he blew her a kiss.

This was the moment to confront him. He would be able to see for himself that she was well, dressed and quite recovered from that stupid fall. She hurried down the hall in the direction of the clatter of dishes in the kitchen, and found Molly bending over an electric range in the spacious, immaculate room which clearly had been modernised from its original state.

'Miss Ayres!' The housekeeper gave a start of surprise. 'You shouldn't be out here you know. Keith said you weren't to get up out of bed until tomorrow!'

'And I say I'm quite all right—and anyway, it's not Miss Ayres, Molly, it's Nicola——' She picked up a heap of cutlery lying on the sink bench. 'Let me set the table for you. Oh, I know,' she added quickly as Molly opened her lips in protest, 'the idea was for me to rest up but I can take it easy here just as easily as in the bedroom as well as,' she smiled her friendly smile, 'see what's going on around the place!'

'I'll see that you take it easy!' Keith was standing in the open doorway, regarding her, and despite the lurking amusement in his eyes, she knew that he meant what he said.

For no reason she was feeling happy and free and well. 'Know what I think?' She twinkled up at him. 'That both of you are scared stiff that I'll flake out again and you'll be stuck with me for another two days!'

Molly said warmly, 'We wouldn't mind, would we, Keith?'

'Guess I could stand it.' Something in the laconic tones lent the words a significant emphasis. 'Right now I'm off to clean up—excuse me, folks!'

Nicola could hear him whistling a tune as he strode down the passage. She felt like whistling herself, she thought, as she went into the big panelled room with its deep easy chairs, worn carpet and carved kauri sideboard and table. A little later when Keith returned to the room she caught the clean fresh tang of after-shave, his thick dark hair was still damp from the shower and his fawn slacks and cream shirt were immaculate. She couldn't seem to keep her eyes from him. And this was the man about whom she had had reservations about sitting beside in a truck, because of his disreputable appearance!

He had moved to the cocktail cabinet in a corner of the room and was setting out glasses. 'What'll you have, Nicola?' Nice to hear her name spoken with that lingering cadence. She was glad she had stopped being 'Miss Ayres'.

Aloud she said, 'A sherry will be fine, thanks.'

'Good. I know Molly's preference. She and I always have a drink before dinner.' He poured the drinks, handed one to her, then went to put a disc on the stereo. The next moment the haunting strains of a native melody, with its melodious Maori voices, stole through the room.

Keith grinned, 'Special for you.'

It was a pleasant meal. Outside the twilight deepened, a star pricked the luminous dark blue of the sky and the pine-covered slopes were in shadow, but overhead the old rose-painted lamp fitted with its modern electric bulb, shed a soft glow over the circular table. Over cold meats and salads, followed by a frothy dessert, Nicola learned something of her host. An only child in the family, he had inherited the home and lands that had long been farmed with sheep and cattle. He, however, had decided to plant trees on the slopes instead of using the land for grazing. Pines, he explained to her, were fast-growing trees and there was an ever-expanding market overseas for the timber. From the port of Tauranga, boats carried shipments of timber to Japan and other parts of the world. Here in Waihi, men were employed in the planting and trimming and felling of the trees and the timber mill provided work for a couple of men. Nicola gathered that since the closing of the gold mines a few years previously, many local men had been thrown out of employment.

Over coffee she mused that he had told her his life history, in a way, but there were no answers to the questions she asked herself concerning him. Had he ever been in love with any other girl, since Janice's death? He was very attractive. Perhaps there was someone he cared for right now—she pulled herself up short. As if it mattered to her!

A little later she helped Molly to clear away the dishes and soon the housekeeper, murmuring something about going to her room, left them alone. It was strange, Nicola thought, curling her feet beneath her on the shabby lounger as Keith put another record on the stereo, how much at home she felt in this house on the other side of the world.

After the last notes died away, a silence fell between them, but it wasn't an awkward silence, she found herself thinking, just companionable and somehow awfully pleasant. If she didn't know better, almost she could imagine this dreamy state of lassitude and well-being had something to do with Keith, which of course was absurd. She scarcely knew the man.

'Penny for them?'

She gave a guilty start. 'Oh, nothing really. I was just

thinking ...' Suddenly she was confused. For something to say she asked, 'Didn't you say you had some old newspapers stashed away somewhere? Maybe I could find something there. You did say a scrapbook?'

'Oh, that,' he grinned lazily. 'If you can stand looking through family records of Lorimers for three generations, starting with the sailing ship they arrived here on from England. There are records of all the highlights in their lives. They were great ones for keeping photos and newspaper accounts of just about everything that happened to any of them. They went through albums like notebooks. There's a stack of them in the office—all the Lorimer tribe, hatched, matched and despatched, as Molly puts it.'

'But you haven't kept it up?'

'Never had the time somehow—or you could say,' the teasing sparkle was back in the dark eyes, 'I've never had anything to put in in the way of a big dramatic event.'

'Like a wedding?'

She couldn't think what had made her say such a thing, but he seemed entirely unperturbed by the question. 'That's right.'

All the same, Nicola chided herself mentally, he would think she was intruding into his personal life and even worse, that she had the matter of weddings on her mind.

'But you never can tell,' he got up to put another record on the spinning disc, 'when something might turn up, something worth recording, that is——'

'How about the pictures of the centenary celebrations, your re-enactment of the finding of gold up on the hill——' She broke off, aghast. What could have possessed her to remind him of that particular event? It was the way he was regarding her, something in his amused glance, that was sending her senses spinning in confusion.

'Oh, that ...' She wrenched her mind back to his calm tones. 'I wouldn't be surprised if Molly hasn't kept the newspaper pictures all ready for Annabel to file away. She's the one who keeps up the family traditions.'

Annabel? Nicola's thoughts were racing. The girl who had been unable to partner him at the ball because of some pressing business of her own that had kept her in town. Suddenly she was very curious about this girl of whom Keith spoke so casually, almost as though she were a sister—but she had been told he had no sister.

She said slowly, 'Is she—one of the family?' She felt ashamed of quizzing him so openly, but somehow she felt she had to know.

'Annabel? Not really. She was brought up with me, our parents were friends. They owned adjoining farms and when her parents died within a year of each other, my folk took her in. She was only a kid then, not even of school age, so we trotted off to school together.' Nicola was busy doing mental arithmetic. She must be around his age, then, this Annabel.

'She's quite a girl,' his eyes were half closed and his deep tones rang with pride. 'You've never heard of Annabel Gowns? No, you wouldn't, having just arrived in the country. She's making quite a name for herself as a fashion designer. She runs a boutique in Auckland, but she travels overseas a lot, picking up ideas and drumming up business, I guess. She's got a good business head, has Annabel.' He grinned reflectively. 'Even though you might not think it, to look at her.'

'Why,' Nicola hoped she didn't sound as curious as she felt, 'is she—attractive?'

Again he gave that enigmatic grin and there was no mistaking the note of pride in his voice. 'I reckon so, and I've grown up with her.'

'You're saying you're prejudiced about her?'

He shrugged broad shoulders. 'You could put it that way. To me she's—well, she's just Annabel.'

Whatever that means, Nicola thought crossly.

'You'll be seeing her for yourself before long,' he was saying, 'she always comes home between overseas trips for a break, just short visits to keep in touch. Saves her sanity, she says, and she's due back for a visit any day now.'

Nicola was silent. For some absurd reason the questions kept going round and around in her mind. He's very fond of her, perhaps more than he realises. Well, proud of her anyway. Is Annabel the reason why he's never married? To push away the thoughts she said, 'Shall we take a look at those old newspapers you told me about? And you did say there was an old family scrapbook I could look through?'

'Right!' He was on his feet in a moment. 'I'll go down to the cellar and see what I can find. Fletcher was the name?'

She nodded. 'Walter Fletcher. He wrote to my aunt from Australia way back in 1960 saying he was thinking of coming to this country. He sent a postcard from Waihi,' she pronounced the Maori syllables carefully, 'and that was the last anyone heard of him.'

'He could have been living and working in Waikino. We'll have a run over there tomorrow and take a look around. It's no distance away.'

Her heart gave a leap of joy. 'What about your work?'

She caught a flash of white teeth in a bronzed face. 'It can wait, when something more important turns up!' All at once his voice took on a serious note. 'You know, Nicola, he'd be getting on a bit by now. Even if you do come across your uncle, you might be in for a shock. He might not be well. Anything could have happened to him in all those years.'

'I don't care,' she set her lips stubbornly, 'just so long as I *know*!'

'There's another possibility too, he was eyeing her thoughtfully, 'has it ever struck you that your uncle might not want to be found? It's just a thought!' he raised a hand in mock defence at her outraged expression, 'but it's one you should face up to. It does happen.'

'Not with Uncle Walter,' she said firmly. 'If you're meaning that he'd done anything against the law, anything to be ashamed of, and that he's been hiding away all these years for that reason——'

'Okay, okay, it was only a suggestion. For all I know, the old boy's the soul of propriety, a harmless old guy who wouldn't hurt a fly!'

'You make him sound as though he's not quite right in the head. He doesn't have to be all that perfect! Come to think of it, he had been mixed up in one or two question-able little episodes, but that was when he was quite young.'

'Oh well, you'll find out about him one of these days, won't you?'

He was making fun of her again, and at the expression in his eyes her annoyance with him fled and she burst out laughing.

'Wait there, and I'll see what I can find!'

He was back in a few minutes, carrying in his arms a huge cardboard carton. 'Sorry to be so long. I had to sort out the recent lot, recent being 1960-65. And it took just as long to get rid of the dust.' He dumped the carton down on the carpet and Nicola dropped to her knees and took out a sheet of yellowed newsprint with its faded heading, *Waihi Times*.

She glanced up at him. 'Did you find the record album too?'

'Right here.' He turned towards an old kauri sideboard and taking out a bound volume, tossed it beside the carton of newspapers on the floor.

'The back sheet of the paper is where we look,' he told her. 'Keep your eyes open for a Fletcher amongst the deaths or the marriages.'

He threw his long length down at her side and presently they were surrounded by newsprint as they went through the back pages of the newspapers. Nicola was finding difficulty in concentrating on the lists of names, for al-though Keith was apparently absorbed in his task of flick-ing through the sheets of newsprint, she was acutely aware of his gaze that was so often fixed on her downcast face.

When at last they came to the final newspaper, she sat back on her heels. 'Well, that's it! We've done our best to find some record of you, Walter de Serville Fletcher, but you seem determined to make yourself invisible, or something.' Her eyes were thoughtful as she began piling sheets of newsprint back in the carton. 'Wouldn't it be funny if he'd gone back to England soon after sending that postcard to Aunt Bella from Waihi? Come to think of it, she always said that her brother loved change and was always thinking up some new scheme of making money quickly without too much effort. Maybe he did strike it rich and——' She broke off, for Keith was staring at her, there was no other word for it.

'Did you say—de Serville?' His tone was no longer laconic but urgent, decisive.

'That's right,' she said, puzzled by his expression. 'It all started with a French ancestor, way back in the family history, and ever since that time, according to Aunt Bella, the eldest son in the Fletcher clan gets lumbered with the name. Why,' her voice quickened, 'do you know someone——'

'No, no. It's an unusual name, that's all.'

She was still perplexed by his interest in the name, but apparently Keith had no intention of enlarging on the matter. She caught his low voice. 'Why didn't I think of it?'

Something about his closed expression stopped the questions on her lips. Instead she asked, 'The family scrapbook you brought up ... could I have a glance through it?' She made a move towards the table but swiftly he stowed the book away in a desk drawer and turned a key in the lock. 'Forget it.'

'But you said——' she eyed him in bewilderment.

'I was wrong. The scrapbook's a write-off so far as you're concerned. All Lorimer family stuff, it wouldn't interest you.'

She had the odd feeling that for some reason she couldn't understand, anything concerning his family would be of terrific interest to her, but she could scarcely hand him that piece of information. She said slowly, 'If you really think so?'

'I do.' How authoritative and definite he sounded!

'The way you said that,' she smiled at him, 'makes me think you've got some guilty family secret that you don't want me to know.'

'Hasn't any family?'

'I suppose so.' What was it her aunt had told her about a family scandal that had been hushed up at the time, something to do with a sum of money missing from a house where Uncle Walter had been staying? She pushed aside the memories. She was becoming fanciful tonight, no doubt about it. Fancy having these suspicions about Uncle Walter! Could she blame the absurd thoughts on the recent effects of concussion? Not really.

'We'll take a run over to Waikino tomorrow instead.' Nicola got the feeling she was being placated like a child offered a treat. 'You never know what you can turn up in the way of records at the School of Mines or the local goldmining museum.' All at once Keith was beside her, so close she could feel his breath stirring the hair at her temples. 'Why don't you sleep on it? Doctor's orders, remember?'

His eyes were gazing deep into her own, his hand moved up to touch her cheek and as a heady excitement possessed her, she knew he was about to kiss her.

The next moment Molly's voice shattered the silence. She was standing in the doorway. 'Shall I bring in some coffee, Keith?'

'No, thanks.' His eyes still held that deep soft look as he stood looking down at Nicola. 'Better get some sleep, Nicola. I'll take you over to Waikino in the morning.'

'Lovely.'

It was pleasant to lie in bed, feeling the soft night breeze blowing over her face, wondering what it would be like to be kissed by Keith Lorimer ... Keith ...

CHAPTER FOUR

In the morning Nicola lay still, listening to a chorus of birdsong that had awakened her and dreamily aware of a feeling of content that pervaded her. She had the oddest feeling of not having started living, not really living, until now. In this exciting unfamiliar existence where each day brought fresh acquaintances and new scenes, why, any-

thing could happen! She decided that she enjoyed playing
detective—especially, a small voice in her mind piped up,
when it involved being with Keith Lorimer!

Keith. Dropping to the floor, she moved to the open
window and stood looking out, breathing in the clear air
with its tang of pines. Along a firebreak in the plantation
of trees, a Land Rover was approaching the house—she
would recognise Keith's dark head anywhere— and hurriedly she moved away. A quick shower and soon she was
pulling a cream cotton skivvy over freshly laundered jeans,
slipping her feet into woven sandals.

As she approached the kitchen she caught an appetising
odour of percolating coffee, eggs and bacon, and found she
was actually hungry. Before coming here she had never
been a breakfast eater. It must be the effect of the pine tang
in the air.

'Morning!' Molly was standing beside the electric range.
'Keith said I wasn't to disturb you, but since you're
here——' She broke another egg into sizzling fat in the
pan. 'My goodness,' she took in Nicola's glowing young
face, 'you look as if you've had a good sleep!'

'Hi, Nicola!' Keith had come into the room, bringing
some magic with him. Or had the day suddenly become
brighter? she wondered. The thought slid through her
mind that if his smile could affect her in this way, she
had best watch herself. He saw her seated, then he looked
at her with his disturbing grin. 'All ready for the big
excursion today?'

'To Waikino, you mean?'

'By jove, she's got it! When it comes to Maori pro-
nunciation, you're improving way out of sight!'

She said smugly, 'I've been practising.'

A little later they went out to the waiting Land Rover
parked near the entrance to the house. Now Nicola could
glimpse the road winding down to fenced paddocks and
a timber mill far below. Strange to think this was her
first glimpse of the exterior of the rambling farmhouse
with its white painted timbers and red iron roof.

'We're away!' Keith slammed shut the heavy door of the

vehicle and they swung down a driveway winding down between dark curtains of pines.

'Did you plant all these?' With a wave of her hand she indicated the symmetrical rows of pines that covered the slope.

He laughed. 'Not me! Those trees take thirty years to mature. The plantation was my dad's idea and I've carried on with the felling and planting of new trees. It's a good way of making use of high slopes not suitable for farming. Down there on the flats I raise cattle.' They rounded a bend and she caught sight of grazing black steers. The lush pastureland was cut by long fences of tall macrocarpa pines and she caught glimpses of stockyards and the mellow red timbers of barns and outbuildings. All at once she became aware of a whine of saws, a sound that increased in volume as they came nearer. 'There's the mill, over to the right,' Keith told her.

Because she had no desire to be reminded of her stupid mistake concerning the Lorimer Timber Company, she said hurriedly, 'Do you cut your own timber from the pine plantations?'

'When it's ready. I also collect timber from farms around the district. Most farmers have a stand of bush that's ready for cutting and that's where I come into the picture. I take along a couple of bushmen and have a bulldozer on the spot to handle the big logs. I take care of the loading and carrying. These days native logs are becoming a rarity, it's a darn shame to fell native bush, but there's always plenty of other timber around for cutting. If you're interested——'

'Oh, I am!'

'I could take you out with me one day and you could see how it's done.'

'I'd like that,' she smiled.

'It's a date, then.'

Even the misty rain that was falling failed to dampen her spirits as they moved into the glistening highway.

Soon the rain became heavier, soaking the punga fronds at the roadside and hitting against the windscreen with silver needles. Banks of cloud hung low and a mist of spray was flung up by passing traffic. As they went on between green paddocks with their grazing sheep, roadside trees were reflected in the wet surface of the bitumen, and always ahead was a range of hills, misty blue in the distance.

Then as suddenly as it had come, the rain cleared away and the sun burst on a newly-washed world. Clusters of fern at the roadside glittered and shone and along clay banks toi-tois, tossing their feathery heads in the breeze, were a translucent freize against a rain-washed sky.

'There's not one chance in a thousand there'll be anything at Waikino that'll help with finding your uncle.'

Nicola, who had been gazing towards the strong masculine profile at her side, came back to the present with a start.

'I know, but it's fun looking. I mean,' she added hurriedly, 'seeing new places and all that.'

'Fun for me too.' Somehow she got the impression that, like herself, he wasn't really thinking about scenery.

All at once the road narrowed between high cuttings in the hills, enclosing them in a shadowed world of soaring cliffs. High above them clouds drifted low over summits of steep rock faces, bare but for gorse with its golden blossoms, and looking upwards, Nicola caught sight of a wire fence suspended in mid-air between steep drops. The road followed the course of a river, swiftly-flowing and choked with great boulders, running beneath the rock walls of the canyon.

Suddenly they were turning into a side road that appeared to lead into thick bush. The next moment, however, a timber building loomed into sight at the roadside and Keith was swinging into a rough gravel driveway to pull up at a hall with a notice 'School of Mines'.

'You never know, I just might come across something here,' Nicola whispered as they made their way towards the doorway. Inside, Keith had a word with the attendant, a quietly-spoken bearded young man, then they were in a shadowy room where logs of timber were burning in an old-fashioned grate. There were few other visitors and it was easy to move around the room, looking at various articles left over from a goldmining era—a miner's candle, a carved wooden spoon, pieces of quartz bearing the glitter of gold, specimens of silver ore, mauve quartz crystals, obsidian.

In another glass case Nicola noticed a tattered wages book with its signatures of miners in days gone by. 'Look,' she drew Keith's attention to the book, 'this might be interesting!' Eagerly she ran her eyes down the lists of signatures—but no, there just wasn't anyone named Fletcher on the list. 'I suppose that would be too much to expect,' she said to Keith, and turned away.

They strolled on amongst the tables of exhibits, pausing to glance at old faded photographs of miners, while Nicola scanned the names beneath the pictures.

In an adjoining room they found gifts and souvenirs, but Nicola's attention was caught immediately by an oil painting hanging in a dark corner, and she hurried across the room to get a closer view.

'It's the gorge we've just come through, isn't it?' She turned a sparkling face to Keith, standing at her side. 'There's the river, boulders and all. Even the day's the same! Wisps of cloud drifting down the rock faces, fitful sunshine picking up the yellow gorse on the bare cliffs. The only difference is a waterfall tumbling down between the bush on a hillside.' For some silly reason she was disappointed. 'So it can't be the same place.'

'It is, you know. I'll show you the view when we leave here. It's just around the bend.'

The dim interior, distant rain falling steadily on misted windows, all conspired to make her feel a heightened sense of intimacy. With a man she scarcely knew? What was the matter with her?

'Would you like to have it?' asked Keith.

'Would I ever?' She spoke out of her thoughts. 'I've never seen a picture that held me like this one does. But goodness, I wouldn't even dare ask the price!'

'If you want it, it's yours.'

'Oh, but I couldn't possibly——'

'Why not? It's in the souvenir department, and you'll want some little memento to take back with you, even if you haven't had any success in the genealogy department.'

Nicola was horrified to realise she had all but forgotten about her original reason for being here. She hesitated. 'I do love it. I don't know how I'm ever going to thank you——'

Keith reached up a hand to take the framed painting from its hook on the wall. 'Just—enjoy it.' He took the picture to the attendant in the adjoining room. 'I'll take this.'

The bearded young man hesitated. 'You do understand that it's rather expensive? Steve McManus is one of our local artists and this is probably the last painting we'll have of his, now that he's making a name for himself overseas. The price——'

'It's all right,' Keith was taking his cheque book from his pocket, 'I'll have it.'

Outside the rain had ceased. 'A clearing-up shower,' Keith told Nicola as he stowed the wrapped painting in the back of the vehicle.

Nicola was wondering why he had given her such an expensive gift. 'If you want it, it's yours,' he had told her. Her heart seemed to miss a beat. Could it be that he cared for her, so soon, so much? Or was she merely dreaming up explanations? Whatever the reason, she could scarcely return the gift he had insisted on buying for her. Better to follow his advice and 'just enjoy it'.

'Wait for it,' he told her as they swung back on to the metal road, 'we're going to hit the town in a minute or so!' They made their way back to the road winding by the river, and soon they had left the shadowed gorge behind and were out in open country once more. As Keith slowed to a stop on the highway, Nicola eyed him in surprise. 'It's not—this is not Waikino?' She glanced towards a handful of dilapidated buildings, one or two of which appeared to be abandoned, with sagging verandahs and peeling paintwork. There was a weathered-looking old hotel no doubt left over from gold rush days, a tiny hut bearing the words Post Office and an old building that had evidently been made into a restaurant. Close by was a small shop, in use as a craft centre.

'Well, anyway,' she said at last, conscious of his amused expression, 'I like it. It's awfully old and abandoned-looking, but it's,' she hesitated and came up with, 'interesting.'

'There's always the waterfall,' he pointed out, 'two of them actually.'

'Let's go and see them, then.'

He started the engine and soon they were following the course of the river once again, passing by an old railway bridge spanning the canyon and turbulent waters beneath. Already Nicola could hear the roar of the falls, then all at once they came in sight of water tumbling endlessly down a bush-clad hill high above. They paused to watch the foaming torrent as it splashed into a rocky pool not far from the roadside, the spray carried by the wind moist on their faces. After a time Keith guided the Land Rover up a rise where higher still, amongst the dense bush growing on either side, white water cascaded over rocks. When at last they turned away Keith asked, 'Where would you like to have a bite of lunch?'

She eyed him incredulously. 'Don't tell me I have a choice, not around here?'

'We have, you know! Remember the restaurant back there in Waikino? It's got quite a reputation for serving good food. Folk come out from town to dine there.'

'What's the opposition?'

'Then there's the craft shop.' They had returned the way they had come and as they came in sight of the low building on the main road, Nicola could discern a painted notice on the window, 'Coffee Shop.'

'Let's settle for the craft shop,' she told him, 'it looks interesting.'

As Keith braked the Land Rover to a stop, two girls rode up on ponies, tethering their mounts on the green lawn adjoining the craft shop. 'Parking provided!' grinned

Keith, and followed Nicola into the shadowy interior. Roughly constructed timber tables and chairs were scattered around the room and hanging on the walls were muslin blouses and kaftans, sheepskin slippers, handtooled leather work and shelves of local pottery.

The coffee, rich and dark, came in pottery mugs and Nicola thought it was delicious. But then today everything seemed a delight. It's because it's all so different, she told herself. Suddenly her life before coming here seemed strangely far away, as if this remote place in the hills *with Keith* were the only reality.

Later, while Keith went to settle the bill, Nicola wandered towards a display of local pottery. Vaguely she became aware of the voices of two middle-aged women seated at a nearby table. 'Isn't that the English girl standing by the pottery stall, the one who's staying at Keith Lorimer's place?'

'Lovely looking, isn't she ... the way she looks at him ... anyone can see ... only hope she won't get hurt. Someone should tell her that any girl who falls for him is asking for trouble. He might like her for a time, but he always goes back to Annabel. The story is that they'll be getting married once she's finished touring around the world getting sales for her gowns.'

Nicola felt a little sick in her midriff. Did it show so much, the happiness she felt in being with Keith? It was only small-town talk, she didn't have to believe the words of two gossipy women. And yet ... and yet ... They were nice motherly-looking women with tanned faces and sensible clothes. Somehow they didn't look the types to make mischief, but being sorry for her was even worse. She pushed the dismaying thoughts away.

The next minute Keith took her arm and they went out into warm sunshine. Overhead only wisps of white cloud lingered in the blue. With Keith at her side, everything was right again, her apprehensive thoughts scattering like the grey clouds that had rolled from view.

His gaze went to a roadside notice: 'One mile to museum.' 'Let's go and take a look!'

They got back in the Land Rover and soon they were strolling up the pathway towards a timber building set against a backdrop of a bush-clad hill. Pushing aside dyed hessian curtains, they moved into a shadowy room where groups of visitors were strolling around the exhibits. Here again, Nicola realised, were the pieces of gold-bearing quartz, the old lamps used by miners working deep in the shafts. It was the collection of photographs of mine workers, however, that held her attention. Her eye ran down the names typed beneath a group of miners pictured.

'It's no use to you,' Keith followed her gaze, 'the date of the picture is way back.'

She turned away with a sigh. 'There must be some way of finding out about Uncle Walter. *Someone* must have known him. If only I could contact some of the old-timers!'

'I can help you there.' There was a glint of amusement in his eyes. 'They're putting on a concert in town tonight, mainly for the old-timers of the district. I could take you——'

She realised he was watching her narrowly. 'What do you say?'

'I'd love to come. Who knows, I just might meet up with someone who knew Uncle Walter.'

'It's an idea.' He seemed ridiculously pleased at her acceptance of the invitation. Almost as pleased as she was. How lucky she was, she mused, to be able to mix business with pleasure like this. For it was a pleasure being with Keith. Could it be because she was alone in an unfamiliar country that she had this deep satisfaction in just being with him, listening to his deep tones as he explained to her something of the history of the goldmining area? Information she didn't always take in at the time because she was too intent on the speaker, finding delight in the bronzed vitality of his face. It was a feeling she had experienced before, of course, while in the company of masculine escorts, but somehow this was different, almost like falling in love.

'They'll be mostly old-timers at the concert tonight,' with

an effort she wrenched her mind back to his deep tones, 'so if you don't mind being with a lot of elderly guys——'

'But you'll be there!'

'I wouldn't miss it!' He grinned towards her. 'I've got a special reason for going, and it's got nothing to do with goldmining.' They laughed together as they made their way back to the waiting Land Rover.

When they reached the house, Keith left her as he went to change into his working gear. Nicola wandered into the kitchen, but Molly didn't seem to be about. The house was very quiet. Strolling out into the back garden, however, she found Molly cutting a crisp lettuce and adding it to the great leaves of silver beet and fresh carrots in the Maori kit lying on the grass.

'Hello,' she greeted Nicola with a smile. 'Enjoy your trip to Waikino?'

'Oh, it was super!' Unconsciously, her face shone with enthusiasm. 'That rocky gorge with the river beneath. And the hills, they seemed to soar up into the clouds. Has anyone ever climbed them?'

Molly's face sobered. 'Lots of folk have clambered up the rock faces and there've been a few accidents there over the years.'

Nicola shuddered. 'I can imagine! In some places a climber would have nothing to hang on to if he slipped and fell. And with the rocks below ... We had a look through the School of Mines and the museum there too.'

'Find anything interesting?'

'Oh, lots of things. Keith got me a painting of the gorge. It's by a man called McManus. Just a souvenir of the visit——'

Molly looked astounded. 'Keith bought you a McManus painting as a souvenir?'

Too late Nicola realised her mistake, for clearly the picture had been an expensive gift. How foolish she had been not to have enquired the price beforehand. She could scarcely return the gift, and anyway she couldn't bear to part with it. Not that she needed any reminder of

today, but it was something Keith had given her, something ... special.

'If you want to find out about anyone who once lived
in the district,' Molly was saying, 'you should have a word
with old Bill. He worked in the mines for years. Now he
lives on the property in a whare up in the hills.' She
pointed to a tiny dwelling on a bush-clad slope a distance
away. 'We see him once a week when he calls in for
bread and mail. He's quite a character really. You should
get Keith to take you over there some time.'

'It's an idea.'

But she had an even better idea. The hut didn't look
more than a mile or so distant and she would be back
at the house before anyone could miss her. She hadn't,
however, counted on running into Molly as she went
through the back gate half an hour later. 'Just taking a walk
over the paddock,' she called airily, and waved a hand in
greeting. Presently she climbed a cleared hill, went down
the other side, then made her way through a fence line
of tall macrocarpas. Immediately, as if at a signal, black
steers converged on her. They came from further down
the slope, ambling towards her with curious eyes. Panic-
stricken, she dodged back between the pine trees. She
wouldn't venture in that paddock again, she vowed silently.
Instead, she made her way along the dividing fence then
struck off in the direction of a patch of thickly-growing
native bush she could see in a gully ahead.

Presently she was in the green gloom of the bush where
tall trees, reaching for the sky, met overhead. It was a
world of filtered light where thick vines twined around
towering trees and densely growing undergrowth made
progress difficult. It was with a sense of relief that she
found a narrow track and she made her way further into
the bush. Somewhere she could hear water trickling and
at times she was forced to go on hands and knees, slipping
and sliding in the damp earth, as she pushed her way
up steep slopes where the greenery had grown over the
old track. Fantails darted around her, flicking from branch
to branch above her head, and the sound of running water

was louder in her ears. All at once she realised that the
track she had been following petered away amongst over-
growing ferns and thorny creepers. She could see no evidence of trampled greenery and decided that a few minutes
ago when she had slid down a bank, she had taken a wrong
turning. But that could soon be rectified. She swung
around and made to push her way through a tangle of
ropes and supplejack, then she paused irresolutely. She
hadn't come this way, that was for sure, then where ...

During the next hour she ventured in various direc-
tions, hopeful that soon she would come across the well-
worn path that old Bill used to reach Sky Lodge. It was
ridiculous, she told herself, she must be close to it all the
time, and yet ... She wiped an arm across a hot face. Her
arms and legs were scratched with thorny creepers through
which she had pushed her way and her hair was damp with
perspiration. There was no sense in blundering on like this.
She realised she was coming very close to panic. She
must be only a mile or so from the farmhouse. There was
no need to feel so ... lost. She knew, because she had
read up the subject before coming here, that there were
no dangerous animals in this country. At that moment an
animal of some sort, crashed through the green undergrowth and she shrank back in terror. The next moment
she caught a glimpse of a goat, then it vanished into thick
bush ahead. She glanced upwards at a massive tree soaring into the blue. Was that the same tree she had noticed
before or wasn't it? She felt a surge of hysteria. Should
she perhaps mark one of the trees? Hadn't she read
of people who, when lost in the bush, had made frantic
efforts to make their way out and only succeeded in coming full circle?

Now stop that, she scolded herself. You can't be that
far from the track and Keith will come looking for you
once he finds you're not at the house. If only she had
worn her wrist watch—but she had no idea how long she
had been blundering on through tangled greenery, sliding
down banks, stumbling over hidden tree-roots and pulling herself up from holes in the ground, hidden by ferns,

into which she had stepped unsuspectingly. Vaguely she
noticed blood trickling down her arm from a deep scratch.
She tied her handkerchief around it, then lost the make-
shift bandage almost immediately. She had no idea how
long she had been wandering on, for time had ceased to
matter and the only thing on her mind was finding her
way out to a clearing, for she had abandoned all hope of
finding the path. Perhaps if she tried this way ...

It was the blood-soaked handkerchief caught on a bush
that brought realisation of the plight she was in. She had
been wandering all this time—why, it was almost dark, and
all she had done was to come full circle, just like those
other lost travellers she'd read about. That was the
moment when the tears came, coursing down her cheeks
to mingle with the dust and sweat. She dashed them away
with the back of her hand as she stumbled on.

'Nicola! Nicola!' At first she imagined she had dreamed
up the thread of sound that seemed so far away, then the
next minute it came again—Keith's voice. He was here,
searching for her. Never had she been so glad to hear any
sound.

'This way!' She had a soft voice, but desperation lent
strength to the call.

'Hold on, I'm coming!' The next moment Keith burst
through a tangle of greenery. To her horror Nicola burst
into tears and threw herself into his arms, sobbing uncon-
trollably.

'I thought you'd never find me and I'd have to stay here
until morning!'

'You should never have come!' His tone, cold and cen-
sorious, jerked her back to some semblance of composure.
His hands were so tight on her shoulders that she expected at any moment to feel him shaking her. 'You
can't keep out of trouble, can you?'

'You're hurting me!'

He loosened his hold on her. 'Don't you know,' his tone
was low with controlled anger, 'that in those light clothes
you're wearing, you could die of exposure in a night spent
out in the open! It doesn't take much—chill, hunger. The

nights are still cold up here and you're just getting over concussion. To think it could have happened to *you*——' With an effort he seemed to gain control of his feelings. 'It was just lucky that Molly happened to mention about old Bill's shack, otherwise I'd still be out with the others, searching through the pine forest. The men have been out for hours.'

Nicola pulled herself free. 'You needn't be like that! I didn't mean to get myself lost, and cause all that trouble to everyone.'

'You're all right?' he enquired belatedly.

'Of course I'm all right,' she said stiffly. 'A bit cold, that's all.' She was shivering. A bit regretful too, she told herself, for causing so much inconvenience, but she hated to admit it to Keith.

'Here, put this on.' He had whipped off his jacket and placed it around her shoulders. For a moment she felt the lingering touch of his hands. 'Feel up to getting along under your own steam?'

'Of course I do. I ...' Her voice trailed away.

'All the same ...' Before she could argue the matter he had swung her up in his arms and clearing a way forward with his foot, began to make his way through a tangle of fern and flax.

'But it's getting dark, you can't see——'

'Not to worry, I know this place like the back of my hand.'

'I must be heavy——'

'Not to me.'

There was something strangely comforting, almost exciting, in being held so close to him, even if he was only carrying her because it made their progress quicker and easier.

'I only wanted to have a word with old Bill,' she said through chattering teeth, 'to find out if he'd ever known Uncle Walter.'

'You would be wasting your time. His memory's shot so it wouldn't make much odds whether he'd ever come across your uncle or not.'

'I suppose so.' It was embarrassing to see how close she must have been to the path all along. When they reached the worn track she imagined Keith would put her down, but he strode on surefootedly—but then of course it was his bush, she reminded herself. She clung to him, her arms around his neck, until they emerged suddenly into a sunset world. 'I can see where we are now.'

He paused in the clearing and she slipped from his arms.

'Come on, then,' he said gruffly, and she wondered if he was still angry with her. She hurried along at his side, waiting as he opened and closed a gate into a paddock, They went over a rise and once again the black steers came rushing towards her, but now she couldn't care less. 'They won't hurt you,' Keith told her, 'they just like to know what's going on.'

As they took the narrow path leading to the back door she asked, 'What time is it?'

'Seven-thirty.'

'Oh. We've still got time to get to the concert in town, then?'

He was silent for a moment. 'I guess so.' He paused. 'You go along inside and I'll pass on the word to the others to call off the search.' In the fading light she caught the glint of reluctant amusement in his eyes. 'You never give up, do you, Nicola?'

Not when it means going out with you. But she kept the information to herself.

Maybe it was because of the night's entertainment with Keith that she felt so few effects of the misadventure, for it was quite amazing what a hot shower could do in the way of reviving tired and aching limbs.

She had been afraid that Molly might have been blamed for her own excursion into the bush, but apparently this was not the case, for the housekeeper seemed concerned only for Nicola's safety.

'You can't blame Keith for being so upset,' Molly told her. Upset? Nicola would have termed his state of mind downright anger. She brought her mind back to Molly's tones. 'He had a young man working for him once, years ago, who wandered away into the bush. When they found him he'd fallen over a cliff and it was touch and go for a while. That would be why Keith kept blaming himself so much tonight, saying it was all his fault for not warning you about wandering into the bush alone. He was quite beside himself, not like him at all. He rang the men who work in the mill and got them out searching right away. One went over by the mill, one up into the pine plantation, and he took the bush track through the gully. Luckily I remembered telling you about old Bill,' she pulled a rueful face. 'I wish I hadn't now.'

'It's not your fault, Molly. Put it down to ignorance and me not knowing the country. I still can't believe I could have come to any real harm in the bush, not in one night.'

Molly's face sobered. 'It's true, though, and what Keith would have done if anything had happened to you, I just don't know. He rushed away to look for you looking as though he had a tragedy on his hands already.'

Nicola couldn't help the thought that maybe his contained anger on finding her to be safe and well had been a reaction to anxiety. He had swung her up in his arms as if she were a length of timber or something, and the way he had spoken to her! Yet during the morning's outing he had seemed so different, so very glad to be with her. She would never understand him. Only like him, prompted a small voice deep in her mind. Oh well, that was different.

She and Keith were finishing the evening meal that Molly had kept hot for them when the telephone rang. Molly came back from answering the call to say, 'It's for you, Nicola—John. He's been trying to get in touch with you all morning, says he wants to ask you if he can take you to the concert in the Memorial Hall tonight. I'll take a message if you like.'

Nicola was about to answer, but Keith didn't give her a chance. 'Give him a message, will you, Molly. Tell him it's too late.' His tone was deep and authoritative. 'You can tell him that she's going with me.'

Nicola had half risen from her seat, but as Molly left the room she sat down again. 'You might have asked me about it!' she said under her breath.

'Why should I?' Apparently Keith was getting back to his usual dominant male self, very much the master of Sky Lodge and all that went on there. 'You said you wanted to come with me.'

'Yes, I know, but——' She shrugged helplessly and decided to let the matter rest. Instead she asked herself what did a girl wear to a concert for old-timers in a New Zealand mining town? More to the point, what did a girl wear on a date with a man who alternately annoyed her to distraction and attracted her wildly?

A little later, when Molly came into the room, Nicola was still trying to decide which dress she would wear to the evening's function.

'You look all right now after your ordeal,' Molly told her with satisfaction.

'Oh, I am! What shall I wear tonight, Molly?' She gestured to the garments laid out on the bed, 'I suppose, for a centenary concert, I should have old-time gear, only I don't have such a thing, only the one-hundred-year-old lace shawl Mrs Hazlett lent me to wear to the ball, and I'm not going to risk harming that!'

'Why not this?' Molly had picked up a creamy skirt with its design of massed pink roses. 'With the muslin blouse——'

Nicola's face cleared.

'Thank you, Molly.' Presently, waiting in the lounge for Keith to collect her, she mused that she could scarcely believe so much had happened to her in one day. A mirror hanging over the mantel opposite reflected her image, the dark hair coiled in a burnished knot, the off-the-shoulder blouse revealing the soft lines of her young body.

Keith, entering the room at that moment, clearly approved of her appearance. 'Nice!' His appreciative gaze lingered on her creamy neck and shoulders, then rose to her face.

Nicola, glancing up to his lean height, thought that he

was undeniably attention-getting himself—the angular
planes of the deeply tanned face, the soft dark hair. The
way in which he was regarding her you wouldn't think he
was angry with her, not now.

'Sorry about today,' his voice was gruff, 'I got a bit
carried away when I found you today. Put it down to a
worrying time, and an outsized sense of relief!'

'Because of me?'

'Because of you.' He smiled the smile that went straight
to her heart. He came to her side and they went out of
the room and with a brief call of 'Goodbye' to Molly,
they left the house. As they neared the Land Rover waiting in the driveway, Keith paused in the starlit darkness.
'You do forgive me?' Before she could make an answer he
had caught her close and kissed her hard on the lips.
Over the leaping of her pulses Nicola had a feeling that
the evening ahead promised to be a joy, old-timers or not!
Yet it wasn't at all a type of entertainment she would have
chosen to go to.

As they swung down the winding driveway, lights beam-
ing ahead in the darkness, she stole a glance towards
Keith's attractive profile and once again she was conscious
of his virility and strength. Aloud she murmured, 'Don't
you think you'll look a little out of place there tonight
amongst the old-timers?'

He sent her a sideways grin. ' Not so much as you will,
young Nicola.'

She laughed. 'Oh, I don't know. Surely there'll be a
few young ones there—John for one.'

'Do you think he'll come, after you turned him down?'

She was surprised. 'Of course he'll be there. He scarcely
knows me.'

Afterwards she wondered if she had merely dreamed up
his low words. 'What difference does time make?'

The hall proved to be an old rectangular building,
ablaze with strings of coloured lights. Inside, the high
raftered ceiling was strung with hanging banners depicting
sketches of old-time miners. The place was crowded and
Keith, taking her arm, piloted her through the throng of

older men in their black suits and old-fashioned waistcoats. Amongst them she noticed a sprinkling of elderly men, gold watch chains looped across their chests, and at the far end of the hall she caught sight of a group of young people, the girls wearing Victorian dresses and poke bonnets, while their male escorts were attired in garments of an earlier age.

Keith found a table near the stage. He brought drinks from the bar, then he and Nicola settled down to listen as local dignitaries mounted the stage to make speeches, mentioning the audience, many of them descendants of families who had emigrated from England, Ireland or Scotland.

'And Australia,' Nicola whispered to Keith.

'If you're lucky!'

Presently the stage lights dimmed and a party of young Maori entertainers ran forward. The women, attractive in their woven flax bodices and swinging skirts, swayed gently as with the inborn rhythm of their race they sang their native songs. Then dropping to the floor and seated one behind the other, they imitated movements of dipping paddles, singing the chants their ancestors had used during the long voyage of the great carved canoes that had brought them across the Pacific to find a destination in these islands of the south seas.

When the party of Maori women had left the stage a buzz of talk broke out in the crowded hall. Keith got to his feet. 'Seeing I promised you I'd do what I could, I'd better get chatting with one or two of the old-timers here.'

Nicola smiled up at him. 'Judging by all the bearded elderly faces, you'll have lots of choice. Good luck!'

He had scarcely begun to push his way through the crowd when a voice said, 'Hi Nicola!' and John dropped down to a seat at the table. 'At last! I've been trying to get in touch with you all day, but you were out a lot.'

'That's right—I was on the trail. It was Waikino this time, going through the museum and the School of Mines——'

'Did you find anything?'

'Not a sign. How about you?' She looked enquiringly into his serious young face.

'I've done quite a bit of research, one way and another.'

'You shouldn't be wasting your working time on my problems——'

'I wanted to do it, and anyway,' an unexpected grin lightened the severity of his expression, 'it wasn't all done in working hours. I managed to get hold of some old electoral rolls of the district, and I went through old deeds and titles, wills, tax records, all that stuff, but I drew a blank every time. If ever he did come to this town——'

'But he did! I've got a postcard sent from Waihi to prove it!'

'Maybe he didn't stay. There were other goldfields opening up in the country at that time, Coromandel for one. You did say he was a restless sort of guy. He could have given it away and moved on. I'm not giving up yet, though, it's possible that someone might remember him and be able to help us.'

Nicola grasped at the idea. 'I know. Keith's making enquiries about Uncle Walter too, that's why we came here tonight. He thought it was worth a try.' Her gaze went to a tall figure amongst the crowd. Keith was obviously deep in conversation with a group of older men.

'Looks as though he's putting the word around.' Then as the lights dimmed and Keith turned to make his way back to the table, John said quickly, 'There's something I wanted to tell you—there's swags of room at home now. Mum said to be sure to let you know we'd love to have you back with us. Keith told me you'd be staying at Sky Lodge all the week, but the way you're looking right now it seems you've made a great recovery from the cliff adventure. We'd like you to come, so how about it?'

Her thoughts were racing. She didn't want to leave Keith's home, she just couldn't bear the thought ... the week was flying by all too fast. 'I did promise Molly,' she heard herself murmur.

'Okay, but if you change your mind, give me a ring at work or at home and I'll come and collect you.'

Change her mind! With Keith doing his utmost to unravel the mystery of Uncle Walter, taking her around the district to show her the wild and rugged beauty of the countryside. 'I'll do that,' she told him, but she knew she hadn't the slightest intention of leaving Sky Lodge one day earlier than she had to.

'I was just telling Nicola,' John said to Keith as he joined them at the table, 'that she's our guest and you've snitched her from us. Kindly return her to us by the end of the week as promised.'

Keith's smiling glance sought her face. His tone was deep and intent. 'That's up to her.' To John he said with a grin, 'Go find your own girl!'

'My own girl?' John's face fell.

'Where is Sharon tonight?' Keith enquired lightly.

'She couldn't make it.' John's tone was muffled. 'See you.' He got to his feet and turned away, but not before Nicola had caught the sudden tightening of his lips.

The next moment she forgot him, for a young Maori girl had run on to the darkened stage, twirling over her head long strings of flax she held in either hand. In the darkness the strings vanished from sight and there were only the tiny balls of green and red swirling in endless illuminated rings. Faster and faster went the music and still the *pois* kept time, tracing their whirling patterns against the blackness of the stage. Now melodious Maori voices took up a traditional melody of the whirling flax balls. '... fascinating thing, tiny balls upon a string.' Nicola found herself keeping in time with her toes to the foot-tapping rhythm. When the item was over and the performer, to a thunder of applause, left the stage, Keith took Nicola around the hall, introducing her to acquaintances and explaining the purpose of her visit here tonight. When they returned to their table she said bewilderedly, 'It's so funny, no one ever seems to have heard of Uncle Walter, yet I know he came here.'

He didn't answer directly.

She was aware of his gaze fixed on her glowing face. 'Tell me, are you glad you came here?'

'Am I ever?' Too late she heard the note of excitement in her tone and added lamely, 'It's all so different.'

'How did you mean?' They were as much alone in the crowded hall as if in a room at Sky Lodge. 'The place, people, way of life?'

But she refused to allow herself to fall into that particular trap again. 'Oh, everything!' She didn't know whether to be glad or sorry as her voice was drowned by two accordion-players seated on the stage.

When the entertainment came to an end Keith escorted her out of the lighted hall and into the street with its long line of verandahed stores and deep ditches on either side of the roadway. As he saw her into the Land Rover the thought flew through her mind that she had known Keith for only a short time, yet she was fast becoming accustomed to his care for her. So much so that she had the oddest feeling that this fascinating and unfamiliar new life would go on for ever.

They sped out of the main street of the town and soon they were passing along suburban areas. As Nicola glanced into the darkness a full moon, struggling from behind banks of clouds, revealed the shadowy outlines of broken stone walls rising against a luminous night sky. 'Scene of the accident,' she commented. 'Doesn't it look a sinister spot by moonlight?'

'Don't you believe it! It was lucky for me!' Keith slipped an arm around her shoulders and as though it were the most natural thing in the world, she nestled close. They passed by the lake of the flooded mine where moonlight threw a shining pathway across the water, the only sound breaking the stillness the plaintive 'more-pork' of a native owl. On and on through the night, the air sweet with the perfumes of flowering shrubs in shadowed gardens. Then presently they were heading up the winding slope towards Sky Lodge, skirting low rows of dark pines, breathing in the tangy air, to come in sight of the house with its lighted front porch.

As they mounted the steps together Nicola said shyly, 'I don't quite know how to say this, but that picture you got for me today, I didn't realise at the time—' she was handling this badly, she knew, 'I've got an idea now that it was awfully expensive.'

He smiled down at her. 'You've got it all wrong. It was like I told you, just a souvenir.'

'I love it, I really do, even though I didn't need anything to remember the day—'

'I'd rather have this!' He caught her close, his dark head bent to seek her lips. Over the wild throbbing of her pulses, his kiss made her lose all count of time or place, everything except the excitement leaping through her.

It seemed a long time later that his voice penetrated her senses. 'That's just to go on with.' He freed her, took her hand in his and they paused at the door. Keith fitted his key in the lock and they went down the passage together. 'Molly must be still up.'

But it was someone else who glanced up as he flung open the door of the lounge room: the most lovely-looking girl she had seen in all her life was regarding Keith with re-proving eyes. It was just, Nicola thought, as if she weren't there at all. 'I thought you were never coming! Molly said you'd gone to the old-timers' social. I couldn't be-lieve it, but she said it was a matter of business.' At last her eyes, wide, green, long-lashed, came to rest on Nicola's face.

'And pleasure,' Keith told her, grinning. 'Nicola, this is Annabel.' Nicola had no need to be introduced to the other girl, for she had known all along the name of the beautiful stranger who appeared to regard Keith as her own property, as no doubt he was.

'Oh yes,' Annabel scarcely spared Nicola a glance, 'Molly told me about you. You're the girl who's out here to try and trace some missing relative. Oh well,' her tone was careless, 'I suppose it's as good a way as any of getting a trip out here for free.'

The colour drained away from Nicola's face. She was

so angry she had difficulty in steadying her voice. 'It wasn't that way at all!'

'Wasn't it?' Annabel seemed uninterested in the subject.

All at once it was very difficult to make clear the true position. How could you, without knowing Aunt Bella's generous nature? And anyway, Annabel hadn't waited for explanations. She had gone to join Keith at the cocktail cabinet. Having already disposed of the sneaky way in which she imagined Nicola had wangled a free overseas trip, she was chatting eagerly with Keith.

He was pouring drinks. 'I know your preference, Annabel—how about you, Nicola? Sherry?'

'Please.'

He handed her the crystal glass, then turned aside to Annabel. 'I didn't expect to see you for a day or two yet. Wasn't business good or did you get through sooner than you expected?'

'Oh, it's been fantastic! The trip overseas really paid off. I've got orders from all the countries I visited. The way things are going,' how confident was the other girl's tone, Nicola thought, 'I'll be starting up another workshop soon. I've worked out some ideas for it already.'

'Good for you.' Keith held up his glass. 'Here's to the new venture!'

The other two went on to discuss the project as if Annabel Gowns were the most exciting subject in the whole world, while Nicola sat playing with her empty glass, forgotten. It didn't matter, she mused resentfully, that she too had travelled across the world for a special purpose; Annabel was interested only in herself. She described the host of attractive, influential men who had vied for her attentions overseas, the wealthy women who had begged her to design for them a dress with the unique 'Annabel' label that set such garments high above her competitors—or so the other girl appeared to think. How could Keith appear so rapt in the one-sided conversation, content to lie back in a deep wing chair and listen attentively as the egotistic tones flowed on—and on—and on?

But of course he would be interested, she would never be
boring to him, for wasn't Annabel the woman he planned
to marry? The scrap of conversation overheard
in the coffee shop earlier in the day, buried deep in her mind
because she hadn't wanted to believe it, now surfaced
with painful truth.

'Actually, I wanted to get back here.' Annabel's confident tones intruded on her musing. 'Not just what you're
thinking!' even Nicola had to admit that the other girl's
smile was really something. 'I had another reason too.
I bet you haven't even bothered to find out that there's a
demonstration of Maori weaving being given here tomorrow, and that's something I must see.'

He looked at her in surprise. 'Don't tell me you're taking
that up now?'

Her laughter trilled out into the stillness. 'Don't be
silly, Keith, you know me! I'll let you into a trade
secret! I've had a super idea for the Gown of the Year
contest I'm working on and I think I'm on to a winner!
The dress I was planning, I've scrapped. This new one
will get me the award, I'm certain of it, if I play my cards
right. I thought now if I design a perfectly simple white
dress, its all in the cut, of course, but it will *look* simple,
then around the hem there'll be a border printed in a
Maori design, the real thing, the *taniko* pattern, you
know?'

He nodded. 'Red, white and black in a sort of conventional
design?'

'That's it. It should look quite dramatic. But I have
to make sure the design really is a traditional one. It all
has to be perfect. So I said to myself,' again the dazzling
smile flashed across her face, 'I'll work things around, alter
my programme so that I can take in the native weaving
display in Waihi—'

'And that was the only reason you came back?' His voice
held an affectionate, teasing inflection.

'Not quite.' Nicola caught the secret glance that flashed between the other two.

She decided she couldn't take much more of this. The

long day, the wine and most of all, a sense of being un-
wanted and in the way, conspired to make her eyelids
droop. 'I think I'll call it a day. See you in the morning.'

' 'Night, Nicola.' They spoke in unison. Secure in their
own Keith and Annabel world, they seemed scarcely aware
of her leaving.

CHAPTER FIVE

NICOLA had expected Annabel to lie in late in the morning,
but when Nicola came into the dining room, she found
to her surprise that the other girl had already prepared
breakfast for Keith.

Her look of blank surprise must have given her away,
because Annabel said matter-of-factly, 'I always get up
early and take over the breakfast when I'm home, isn't that
right, Molly?'

'That's true!' Molly, busy with the vacuum cleaner in
the open doorway, yelled back. Why must everyone in
the house defer to the other girl? Nicola wondered resentfully.

'He knows no one else can whip up an omelette just the
way he likes it,' came the smug, self-satisfied tones. 'I don't
bother for myself—I never eat breakfast. Not that I need
to worry, I seem to stay slim no matter what I eat—shall
I put a piece of toast on for you, Nicola?'

'If you please.' Nicola was wishing she had delayed
her entrance to the breakfast table until Annabel had left
the room, but it was too late now. She seated herself at
the table, aware of deflated feelings and hoping Annabel
wouldn't notice her heavy eyelids following a sleepless
night.

A little later she was alone at the table, nibbling dis-
piritedly at a piece of toast, when Molly came into the
room. She helped herself to coffee and seated herself
beside Nicola.

'I have a holiday from getting breakfast when Annabel's at home,' she said.

'She told me she always gets Keith's breakfast for him, when she's here.' There was a poignant sweetness in just speaking his name.

Molly sipped her coffee. 'She's always so busy when she comes home. The telephone never seems to stop ringing. She says it's a good chance for them to be together, and catch up with the news. They always seem to have so much to talk about, those two, especially this time.'

Nicola raised her brooding glance. 'Why this visit in particular?'

Molly looked surprised. 'Didn't they tell you? They're so full of their plans I thought they would have let you in on them, but of course there hasn't been much time.'

Nicola felt a pang shoot through her and it was with an effort that she wrenched her mind back to Molly's satisfied tones. 'I enjoy the break from getting evening meals too when Annabel is home,' Molly went on. 'Usually Keith takes her out to dinner somewhere in town. I wonder why——' Her brow cleared. 'I suppose it's because you're here that they're staying in this evening.'

Nicola writhed inwardly. So she was playing gooseberry to lovers here at Sky Lodge, but not for long! She hardened her heart, telling herself she must get over this stupid weakness for Keith, and she would! Ever since Annabel's arrival at the house she had known there was no place here for her. Now she had made a decision. She would ring John and ask him to come and take her back to his home now that their visitors had left the house and there was room for her.

During the next hour it seemed to Nicola that Annabel was everywhere at once, planning an evening menu for Molly to prepare, leafing through sketch books of fashion designs, scattering overseas magazines over the carpet, trailing lengths of material from room to room. 'What do you think of this one, Keith?' she appealed to him as he came into the room, a length of shimmering fabric draped around her slim body.

Nicola saw him give the other girl a quizzical smile, heard his deep, amused voice. 'Not much.'

Annabel shot him an exasperated glance. 'Oh, you're impossible! Trouble with you is that you've no fashion sense! I bet you'd like me just as much if I were wearing some corny outfit bought off the peg, exactly the same as every other girl in the country is wearing.'

Like me? Nicola wondered uneasily if the words were an oblique reference to her own faded blue jeans and simple white cotton top.

Keith said easily, 'Now that you two girls are getting to know each other, I've just had a thought. Annabel, seeing you're off to the Maori Craft Centre today, how about taking Nicola along with you? The native way of weaving flax will be all new to her. So far the only idea of Maori culture she's had has been a *poi*-swinging display and a few Maori songs she heard at the concert the other night.'

'I really don't think——' Nicola was about to make an excuse, any old excuse that would keep her from going with Annabel, when the clear forceful tones forestalled her.

'I don't think she'd get anything out of it. Maoritanga wouldn't mean a thing to anyone who's just arrived in the country.' She tossed Nicola a careless glance. 'Believe me, you wouldn't enjoy it.'

All at once Nicola was sick and tired of being pushed around by Annabel. A moment previously she hadn't wanted to go anywhere with the other girl, but perversely she refused to have her mind made up for her in the matter. She lifted her chin and said quietly, 'I'd like to see the display.'

'How long are you staying with us, Miss Ayres?' Annabel's question took her by surprise.

'Just until tomorrow.' She avoided Keith's look of astonishment. She had made the decision at that moment. She wouldn't stay around here while these two ... She would contact John by telephone and ask him to call and take her away. Already she had stayed far too long for her own peace of mind.

She became aware that Keith was regarding her thoughtfully. 'I was hoping you would stay until the weekend, but if you'd rather——'

'I have to go.' I must, because the sight of you and Annabel together is something I can't take.

He said coolly, 'Just as you please, it's up to you.'

Back in her room Nicola threw herself down on the bed and stared up at the ceiling. The brittle happiness of yesterday had been shattered, leaving only a dull ache of hopelessness. Could this be love? But she had known Keith for such a brief time. Long enough for his dark forceful face to be with her constantly, long enough for her to find delight in the sound of his voice. Maybe, she told herself forlornly, once she was away from the heady magic of his nearness, she would get over this madness, blot from her mind the burning memory of his kiss. Only a kiss. How could she have guessed that a kiss could light up your life and make everything else in the world seem of little importance?

The echo of Keith's footsteps as he strode along the path beneath her window roused her from her musing and she crept along the hall to the telephone.

'Nicola!' The note of delighted surprise in John's tone brought a measure of solace to her bruised feelings. He sounded inordinately pleased to hear from her and even more delighted with the news that she wanted to return to his home. 'I'll pick you up on the way back from work,' he promised.

In her room once again she wandered listlessly about, taking garments from the wardrobe and placing them in her suitcase. Then she stood motionless, the oil painting of the Waikino gorge held in her hands. She would always treasure the picture as a memento of an unforgettable day. Why, she wondered, had Keith given her such an expensive gift? There was no answer to the question, and with a sigh she placed the picture carefully beneath a pile of folded garments. Her packing was soon completed and she paused irresolutely. But you couldn't stay here for ever feeling sorry for yourself. Sorry? Or mad with yourself for being so naïve as to imagine for one moment that Keith could have for her the feeling that, why not admit it, she had for him. At any moment now Annabel would be leaving for the craft centre, and although she had no wish to accompany the other girl, she was determined not to change her mind.

When she entered the lounge Annabel was waiting for her, looking more attractive than ever in a deceptively simple cream pants suit with accents of emerald green. The cap of smooth and shining blonde hair, the perfect figure and above all, the other girl's air of complete confidence all added up, Nicola thought, to someone irresistibly appealing. But then, the thought slid into her mind, Annabel was no longer a girl. She had had many years in which to acquire a personality that radiated charm and self-esteem. When it came to Nicola, however, the charm didn't seem to operate. 'You won't enjoy all that Maori stuff,' Annabel said repressively.

'All the same,' Nicola's soft lips were set in a stubborn line, 'I'd like to go to the craft centre.'

Annabel shrugged. 'Come on, then,' she said ungraciously.

Nicola's heavy feeling of heartache persisted as she slid into the small car with its violent paintwork and fluffy sheepskin seat covers. The brilliance of the New Zealand sunlight revealed tiny lines fanning out from the corners of Annabel's big green eyes, but she was still the most lovely woman Nicola had seen in all her life. No wonder, she mused wistfully, that Keith wasn't aware of anyone else when Annabel was around.

As they swung down the winding road skirting a dark curtain of pines, Annabel talked of the Gown of the Year contest which she was entering with high hopes of being the winner. Now, however, Nicola was glad of the other girl's absorption in her own affairs. The endless stream of talk left Nicola free to pursue her own thoughts, and at least she was spared the effort of making conversation. Idly she wondered that Annabel, with her spectacular blonde beauty, hadn't married long ago, but she flinched away from that line of thought. It opened up too many hurtful possibilities.

It wasn't until they turned into the main road that Annabel spared a thought for the girl seated silently at her side. 'Keith said you've only been in the country a short time. How did you come to meet up with him?' Her eyes said, 'And how come that you, a stranger, are staying in his home?'

Nicola roused herself from her unhappy musing. 'I had an accident and Keith happened to be the one nearest to the scene of the trouble when I took a header down an overgrown cliff. He took me to the local doctor and seeing he prescribed rest for a day or so——'

For once, Nicola thought, the other girl appeared to be thinking of someone other than herself. 'Lucky for Keith!'

Unlucky for me. But she said the words under her breath. She liked him far too much, this Keith Lorimer of the mocking smile and all-too-perceptive eyes.

'Tell me,' she became aware of Annabel's clear tones, 'you were in London just a short while ago. What was the fashion scene like over there?'

Nicola considered. 'Not much different from what girls are wearing over here, actually. From what I saw of the Auckland boutiques in the short time I was there, they're fairly up-to-date with their ideas.'

'I think so too. When I was over in London last year at a fashion conference——' Nicola was only half aware of Annabel's voice as the other girl went on to describe her many successes overseas. Was she referring to personal friendships, love affairs, fashion shows? Nicola had lost the thread of the narrative.

Presently they were approaching a Maori meeting house with its crossed beams carved in scrolls and grotesque squatting figures with gleaming paua-shell eyes. In the dim interior of the raftered room the two girls watched native women splitting long lengths of green flax with mussel shells.

'What I'm here for,' Annabel was saying, 'is to get the feel of it all. It might make all the difference to my fashion entry, and Maori weaving and dyeing with mud and tree-bark is an art that's fast disappearing.' Her tone was impersonal, almost friendly—but then, Nicola thought bleakly, Annabel had no cause to fear the stranger as a rival for Keith's affection. A stupid girl who kept making all manner of mistakes in an unfamiliar country and getting herself into awkward situations. Keith's words echoed in her ears. 'You just can't keep out of trouble, can you, Nicola?'

Presently they strolled towards a group of Maori women who were weaving patterns from flax dyed in colours of red white and black. 'It's the *taniko*, the traditional pattern,' Annabel explained, and taking a notebook and ball pen from her bag, she began to sketch the geometrical design.

Nicola wandered away, pausing to watch other groups of women who were laughing and chatting together as brown-skinned fingers deftly wove strands of flax into baskets and skirts. At another stall she stopped to buy tiny balls of flax she recognised as the *pois* used on stage at the local concert she had attended with Keith. For something to do, she twirled the two balls on their long strings high in the air, only to find they were hopelessly tangled.

At that moment she became aware of Keith, who was making his way through the groups in her direction. Nicola could feel the hot colour flooding her cheeks as he neared her. 'It looked so easy when the girls at the concert twirled the *pois*.' She gave up trying to untangle the strings.

The warm amused light lingered in his eyes. 'It's easy, once you know how. You should get Annabel to give you some lessons one day. She's a wizard on the *pois*.'

She would be, Nicola told herself silently. Was there any skill, from whipping up an omelette to twirling tiny balls of flax in the air, at which Annabel didn't excel?

'Hi, Keith!' She became aware of the other girl's clear tones as Annabel strolled towards them. 'What brings you along here today?' She raised a provocative smiling face. 'I never knew you to have the slightest interest in weaving.'

'I haven't!' He challenged her laughing gaze. 'Guess again!'

Nicola turned despairingly aside. No need to spell it out. Clearly he couldn't bear to allow Annabel out of his sight. What was it that Molly had said about them? 'Annabel is the only one he really *cares* about.' That was the moment Nicola was thankful that she had arranged to leave Sky Lodge, glad that she had somewhere where she could go, seeing the town was overtaxed as regards accommodation.

'Did you get what you wanted in the design department?' Keith was asking Annabel.

She opened her sketchbook in a flash. 'Just what I was looking for. I'll use this design for my dress for the contest. A border all around the hem in the traditional red, white and black.'

He glanced carelessly down at the pencilled sketch. 'Should be fine.'

Annabel smiled up into the dark masculine face. 'You haven't an idea of what I'm talking about, have you?'

At long last he looked towards Nicola, *really* looked at her. It was a glance that took her by surprise, deep and tender and loving, the way she would have imagined he would be looking at Annabel. After all, it was the other girl he had come to see. His words, however, were ordinary enough. 'What did you make of it all, young Nicola?'

'It was very interesting.' If only he wouldn't look at her that way! She couldn't seem to collect her confused thoughts. 'And I did *try* to learn to twirl the *pois*.'

'Good for you!' Could it be the shadowy interior of the room that lent his eyes that deep soft look?

'You should practise with the *pois*,' Annabel told her. 'You'll soon pick it up. I'll show you how if you like. You might find it handy to trot out as your Kiwi accomplishment when you get back to your home village. That is,' she added carelessly, 'if you ever do go back there.'

'Not go home?' Nicola was puzzled. 'Why shouldn't I?'

Annabel's considering glance rested on Nicola's flushed

young face. 'Oh, nothing, just that you never know your luck, husband-wise!'

'I'll take you up on that,' Keith's deep tones cut in, 'at odds of ten to one!'

Nicola's thick lashes dropped to hide the pain that clouded her eyes. Why must these two discuss her affairs as if she were a hundred miles away? She gathered herself together, lifted her chin and said, 'Like I told you, the only male that I'm interested in over here is my Uncle Walter (*liar*)—if there *is* an Uncle Walter still around some place.'

'If you say so,' said Annabel, and flashed her disbelieving smile. She turned to Keith. 'Seeing you're here ... I'm off to town to look up some of the old crowd. How about you, Nicola?'

She shook her head. 'Thanks all the same.' The other girl had made it perfectly plain that she wasn't wanted. Well, that suited her. All she wanted just now was to escape from Annabel's reluctant company.

'Take Nicola along with you, will you, Keith?'

Ridiculous to feel this tide of happiness surging over her at the commonplace suggestion. She knew it was madness for her even to be thinking of him, but somehow she couldn't help herself.

A little later, as they turned off the main road, from her high seat in the cab of the timber truck, she asked, 'Where are we going?'

'To a farm up in the hills. I've got to pick up some timber, the men are working there today.' The grin he tossed her made the day suddenly seem brighter. 'All right with you?'

'Oh yes, anywhere does me.' *Anywhere that's with you*, the voice in her mind reminded her.

Soon they were taking a rough track leading up into the hills and there was only an occasional milk tanker or farm lorry on the winding dirt road. Ahead of them, violet shadows lay on bush-clad slopes away from the sun. The air was so fresh, a champagne day! Nicola decided she liked this new land, what she had seen of it. Because of her enquiries in the district she was of course more or less confined to this part of the country. Oddly, she didn't seem to mind.

Because the silence was becoming somehow intimate, she heard herself say, 'I'm not having much luck with Uncle Walter. I had a phone call from John yesterday——'

'John?' How odd was his tone, so quick and almost suspicious. 'What did *he* want?'

'Nothing much. He just wanted to tell me that he'd made some enquiries. It was good of him to go to all the trouble just for me——'

'What sort of enquiries?'

'Oh, you know, electoral rolls, the sort of thing a lawyer might have access too.'

'I get it.' Keith's tone had lost the terse note and he seemed to relax.

'But he didn't find a thing. It's just as though that elusive uncle of mine had never lived in Waihi at all. But that couldn't be right,' she was speaking her thoughts aloud, 'or he couldn't have sent the postcard from here.'

'Probably left right afterwards and never came back.'

'But then why didn't he ever write? Not even a Christmas card, in all those years. He *must* have died.'

'You know something, Nicola?' The way Keith spoke her perfectly ordinary name sent her senses flying into confusion and she had to force herself to think very hard about Annabel. She wrenched her thoughts back to his voice.

'You've done your best to trace him in the mining district around here. Why not call it a day and leave it at that? For the rest of your time here, why not just— enjoy yourself.'

She stared across at him in surprise. 'But I couldn't give up already! I just can't go back and say "sorry, Aunt, it was too hard, so I gave up the idea." ' She added teasingly, 'Are you trying to get rid of me?'

'Would I do that? Seriously though, don't you see, you'll be wasting all the time you have here on a wild goose chase.'

'I like chasing wild geese, and I am enjoying myself.'

'You seem to fit in with Kiwi ways pretty well, young Nicola.'

She pulled a face. 'Why do you call me that? I'm not all that young.'

'How young, then? Eighteen?'

'I'm twenty-one. It's the round childish face that gives everyone the wrong impression,' she complained. 'I have to keep explaining.'

'I'd say you were just the right age.'

She flung him a swift glance, but he was gazing ahead, his attention with the long beer tanker he was passing on the narrow road. She had been about to ask, 'The right age for what?' then just in time she remembered Annabel's careless tone. 'Take Nicola along with you, will you, Keith?' Like a dog, or a parcel. Just in case you're getting any romantic notions about this little trip, she reminded herself, don't forget that he's merely going about his ordinary work. He didn't even plan to take you with him!

'I often come out this way,' the vibrant tones jerked back to the present. 'Farmers with small stands of timber sell it to me and I go out and cut and transport it.' They were swinging into a rough track bulldozed through a bush-filled gully where tall trees reached for the sky. Presently the whine of a chain saw fell on the still air. At last they pulled up on a tree-shadowed pathway and Nicola's gaze went to a stand of trees nearby where a man was wielding a chain saw. Close by, another man was hauling down a tree with a heavy tractor. They were powerful-looking men, deeply tanned, wearing black sweat shirts and tattered shorts. Keith waited until their work was completed, then went to speak with the bushmen. From her seat in the truck Nicola watched as Keith and the two men spoke together. Soon he came back to join her. He put the engine into gear, drove alongside a bank and with the help of the bushman, rolled the long lengths of timber from skids to his truck.

A little later he was back in the truck beside her.

'So now, I suppose, it's back to the sawmill?' Nicola

turned to wave goodbye to the men standing against a backdrop of bush-covered slopes.

'You've got the idea.'

As they lurched along the bush track she asked idly, 'What were they laughing about? And don't try to tell me it was nothing to do with me, because I could tell it was by the way they were looking at me.'

He grinned. 'Do you really want me to tell you?'

'I'm asking you.'

'It was nothing much,' they bumped over a hidden tree root on the track and she was flung against him. 'They wanted to know how come a girl like you was in the district and they hadn't heard.'

She eyed him suspiciously, a smile curving her lips. 'Is that all?'

'Not quite. They accused me of being too mean to let you out of the cab, said I was trying to keep a good thing to myself.'

She burst out laughing, 'How absurd could they get!'

To her surprise he didn't even smile. 'Thing is, young Nicola, they've known me a lot longer than you have. I'm jealous as hell and they know it!'

He must be joking, he *must* be, for jealousy implied warmth of feeling even—love, all the emotions she longed he would feel for her instead of Annabel.

Because it hurt to think of the other girl she changed the subject, plying him with questions concerning the trees towering around them. Many were native varieties, he explained, growing nowhere else in the world and attaining their height and girth in an incredibly short span of time. He was a timber man and she knew she had struck a topic close to his heart and, deep in his subject, he seemed unaware of her silence. Nicola was thinking that she now had her chance to feast her eyes on the strong masculine profile at her side. She had just made a discovery that she liked a man to have a strong chin, especially a sun-bronzed chin with a dent!

As they climbed higher the thickly wooded slopes gave way to cleared paddocks and from her perch beside the driver she gazed around her, taking in the green hills dotted with grazing sheep and wisps of cloud drifting by.

Far below, Waihi lay bathed in sunshine, a toy town with miniature houses half hidden amidst surrounding greenery.

'It's good farmland up here in the hills,' Keith told her, 'though a lot of the slopes have been left in bush or planted in pines.' He was guiding the truck into a rough track and soon they were lurching over rough ground towards a clearing in a cluster of tall leafy trees. 'We're here!' Switching off the engine, he jumped to the ground and came around the vehicle to fling open the door of the cab. 'Can you jump?'

For answer she dropped from the high seat, to be caught in strong arms. For a timeless moment he held her close, then he set her gently down. The next moment he had moved back to the truck while she remained motionless, her heart beating crazily. It was very still, the only sound the piping of insects in the bush around her, a tui's musical note echoing from somewhere in a high tree. All at once Nicola had the oddest, dreamlike feeling, as if they two were alone in the world, a man and a woman getting to know each other, getting to love—Love? She pulled herself up short. She must be out of her mind!

She realised he was looking at her intently, watching her as she dropped down to the warm grass, hands linked around her knees.

'Tell me about yourself!' He was kneeling at her side.

'Me? What do you want to know?'

'What you've been doing with yourself, all these years before we met?'

Before we met. What an odd way to phrase the question. Almost as though it were somehow important that he should know. There she went, dreaming again. Aloud she murmured, 'Oh, nothing that you'd be interested in. Just living, just living.'

'How do you know it wouldn't interest me? Start at the beginning and take it from there.'

'The beginning?' She gave her soft, low laugh. 'An orphan—does that sound pathetic to you? It isn't really. My aunt brought me up when my parents were killed in an accident. She's a darling. It was Aunt Bella who sent me out here on this holiday——'

'Holiday?' Keith raised quizzical eyebrows.

'Well, it's a sort of holiday. Where was I? The beginning, you said? It was just the usual pattern—school, college, then commercial training that landed me in a lawyer's office in a small town where I live in Lincolnshire. That's how I came to have a letter of introduction to the Hazletts. My boss——'

'Never mind about the Hazletts. It's you I'm interested in hearing about. Office work? Well, that would take care of the days. How about the nights, weekends. Any hobbies, interests, what have you?'

'Nothing that's wildly exciting. I play tennis, make all my own clothes ...' Her voice faded into silence. She had a mental picture of Annabel's sketchbook with its fashion design for her entry in the Gown of the Year contest. She hated herself for the deprecating note in her voice as she added, 'Not like Annabel, of course.'

'That cream dress you wore to the ball the other night——?'

'Oh yes, that was all my own work.'

'Well then——' The appreciative glint in his eyes did a lot towards restoring her flagging confidence. She had always taken a pride in her home dressmaking, until now. Why did Annabel affect her in this way? It was ridiculous, it was becoming a habit with her.

'Go dancing?' His voice jerked her from her musing. Goodness knew why he was putting her through this questionnaire, but—— The corners of her lips twitched slightly; she didn't have to go into details of her life in England. 'Sometimes.'

'So'—swiftly he followed up his advantage, 'I take it there's no interesting men in your life right now?'

She caught her breath. If he only knew the answer to that one! With an effort she schooled her voice to a note of amusement. 'I wouldn't be here if there were, do you think?'

'Just what I'd figured out for myself!'

But there was someone else in his life, someone who mattered a great deal. The thought came unbidden.

'Now that we've got that sorted out,' all at once he was gay and carefree, 'what do you say to a tea-break?'

'I'd like that,' but she spoke absently. Annabel was his love. Whatever magic the day held for her, to him she was merely a pleasant diversion, someone with whom he could fill in the time while Annabel, busy, sought-after, clever Annabel, was elsewhere.

'What's wrong? Afraid of the bush?' He was sauntering towards a blackened patch of the grass, a short distance away. He glanced back and tossed over his shoulder, 'There are no wild animals around here, except maybe the odd wild pig, and he won't be looking for company.'

'I guess I'm just thirsty.'

How could she confess to him that she was afraid of her own emotions, the feelings that were leading her in the direction of falling in love with a man who was already deeply involved with another girl? She remembered his wager of ten to one that she would marry a New Zealander and never return to her homeland. That was about how much she counted in his scheme of things, a proof, if she needed one, of his attitude towards her.

'Ever tasted billy tea?'

'Not yet.'

'Now's your chance, then! It's got a special flavour, sort of smoky and outdoorish but guaranteed to quench the meanest thirst!' As he spoke he was gathering up dried branches lying on the ground and Nicola went to help him. Soon he was setting a match to the sticks and she watched the flames licking around a blackened billy. In no time at all, it seemed to her, he had made tea, adding a twig of tea-tree, and pouring the steaming brew into plastic mugs.

'How is it?' He was squatting at her side, watching as she took a sip of the dark brown liquid.

'It's ... different.'

'Is that all you can say?'

'And smoky—but I like it that way,' she added hurriedly.

'Have a sandwich to go with it!'

'A sandwich?' She looked up at him in surprise. 'Such luxury! Molly must be looking after you well!'

'Oh, she does!'

Nicola munched contentedly, her face flushed with the flames, while smoke from dying embers rose lazily in the warm clear air. After a moment she murmured contritely, 'It's your lunch that I'm eating.'

'Only half of it.'

When they had shared the last sandwich between them, Keith glanced towards her with the teasing, enigmatic look she was beginning to recognise. 'Tell me,' he put up a hand to twirl a long strand of her dark hair around his fingers, 'would it worry you if you never went back to England?' His voice was lazy. 'I mean, there's no special man you're missing a lot, over there?'

'I told you,' she said very low, 'no——'

'In that case——' Suddenly his tone was no longer relaxed but excited, tinged with urgency. He made to draw her close, but she had sprung to her feet.

She was trembling, but whether from anger or his nearness she couldn't have told. How could he, *how could he*, loving Annabel as he did, try to make love to her? Just because they were alone here together, just because she happened to be passably attractive.

'What's the matter?' He was angry, she knew. It showed in the taut line of his mouth, the smouldering expression of his eyes. 'Don't worry,' his voice was ice-cold, 'I must have got the wrong impression.' He strode away to fling the billy in the back of the truck. He tossed the mugs into a box, and returned to fling cold water on the glowing embers. 'A while ago I could have sworn you weren't exactly hating me.'

'I don't,' her voice was very low, 'but that doesn't mean——'

'Doesn't mean I can kiss you. Is that it?'

'How many girls do you like to keep on hand?' The next moment she was glad he hadn't caught her low words.

'Don't worry,' his tone softened, 'if that's the way you want it. My mistake, I guess. I got the idea you rather liked me——'

'I do, but you——' She stopped short. How to find the words to tell him how she felt about him? But you love someone else! He would think she was crazy, talking about love. Just a kiss ... How to explain that she didn't want light kisses while his real love was far away? If she couldn't have his whole heart, be the one girl in the world for him, she didn't want to be close to him. Didn't want—or didn't dare? She tried to push the betraying thoughts aside. *Coward*. You know if you surrender to his caresses, you'll be more than ever in love with him, she thought. Survival tactics, that's all you're playing at. Why not admit that you're trying to save yourself a lot of heartache, opting out while you can?

Across the tumult in her mind flashed a new thought. He wouldn't understand how she felt about him. To him she would be merely a girl who enjoyed leading men on until she tired of the game.

All at once he was close behind her, his arms around her shoulders, his face pressed close to hers. 'Why are you trembling? I wouldn't do anything to hurt you for the world—*you* of all people! It was just a kiss that I had in mind.'

Just a kiss. Gently he turned her face until she was looking up into his eyes, and this time she didn't try to run away. His mouth was on hers and the world slipped away. It seemed a long time before she became aware of everyday things, heard the double note of a tui echoing from a tree high above.

Abruptly he released her. 'Shall we go?' His voice was cool, controlled. If only, she thought wildly, he didn't realise the effect his kisses had on her.

On the way back to the house on the hill, they spoke

little. But below her composed manner Nicola's thoughts were whirling. So this is love, this pain and longing and hopelessness, for a man who thinks little of light kisses when the opportunity arises. If only I felt the same way! But I don't and I never will. Even though I know he isn't worth loving, somehow it makes no difference. If I could I'd put him right out of my mind, she thought. At least I can get away from Sky Lodge while I've still a shred of sanity left.

When they reached the house she busied herself helping Molly in the kitchen. Almost she found herself envying the older woman with no heartache to disturb the even tenor of the days, her only problem the evening meal. Would she ever be free of Keith, free of the longing?

'Peel a few apples for me, will you, love, and I'll pop on the crust.' Molly's blue eyes twinkled. 'There's one thing I've learned about men over the years and that is if you want to please them you can't go wrong with serving apple pie for dessert!'

'Keith too?' In her present state of mind there was a poignant pleasure in talking of him.

Molly nodded. 'I found that out the first week I was here.'

When the evening meal was over, because it hurt to see Keith and Annabel seated close together in the lounge, chatting and laughing together so intimately, Nicola escaped to the kitchen and helped Molly with the dinner dishes.

When she returned to the lamp-lighted room, she found Annabel and Keith seated on the floor, examining sheets of architectural plans scattered over the carpet. The two heads, one blonde, one dark, were close as the two bent over the tracings.

Nicola picked up a magazine and pretended to read, but the voices stabbed her consciousness.

Keith's voice, 'I'm not too happy about the pitch of the roof. And how about if we make this room a foot bigger, put a window on the back wall?'

Annabel's excited laughter. 'But that's marvellous! Why

didn't I think of it before? It takes two to work out the perfect house plan. I'll ring the architect tomorrow and get him to draw up a new set of plans.'

'Tremendous! And while you're on the job, how about an open balcony here, off the master bedroom? We can still use the original timber.'

So that was it, Nicola thought, heavy-hearted. The plans were in connection with the modernising of the present house. If she had needed any further proof that the other two were planning marriage and a home together, she had it now. If only it didn't hurt so much!

It was a relief when at that moment the telephone bell shrilled through the room and Molly came back from answering the call. 'For you Nicola, it's John Hazlett.'

The thoughts rushed through her mind as she hurried away. Supposing the Hazletts couldn't put her up at their home after all? The next minute, however, John's measured tones allayed her suspicions.

'Just checking up to make sure you're all set for to-morrow.' He was the type of man who would always make doubly sure of arrangements.

'Yes, everything's still the same.' She laughed. 'I could come right now if it suited you better.'

'Funny you should say that.' She caught a note of relief in his quiet tones. 'Actually it would suit me fine. I've had an urgent call to be in court all tomorrow, so if you could make it tonight instead, say in half an hour's time?'

'I'll be ready.'

'I think I might be on to something about your uncle,' she could picture his serious intent expression, 'but it's all a bit up in the air at the moment.'

'Really?' She forced a note of enthusiasm into her voice. Somehow she couldn't summon up a great deal of interest in the matter. When she had first arrived in the country, such a short while ago, she had imagined that nothing could deflect her from her purpose. It had taken a man to do that, a man who felt no real affection for her. She wrenched her mind back to the even tones.

'I had one reply to the ad I put in the district news-papers. I'll show it to you when I see you.'

'Tell me now!' Anything to take her mind from a man and a woman who were busy with their house plans in the adjoining room.

'There's not much to tell. It seems this family of Fletchers, they live out at the coast, by the way, had a relative from Australia come to stay with them when they first moved into the district. His name was Walter and they've got a letter of years back and an old photograph, but that's all. They've never kept in touch through the years, but they're making enquiries from the rest of the family. They seem a nice crowd, insisted that I bring you out to see them at the weekend, so we can talk it over.'

'Lovely!'

'See you soon, then.'

Slowly Nicola replaced the receiver. It wasn't lovely at all, that plan of John's to take her out to the coast at the weekend and to pick her up from Sky Lodge tonight. It was a wrench to force herself to leave here, yet she knew with inner certainty that each hour she spent beneath the same roof as Keith meant storing up heartache for herself. Somehow she must engross herself in other interests. After all, she asked herself, what's so special about this one man? The answer came unbidden. He's everything I could wish for in a man, and he's in love with Annabel! How did one find a cure for heartache? Another love affair? But other men held no appeal for her, not now. All she could do was to concentrate on other matters, especially the reason that had brought her half way around the world. Oh, Uncle Walter, if only I'd known what I was letting myself in for when I went searching for you! she sighed.

When she got back to the lounge the other two were still intent on their plans.

Keith looked up. 'Know anything about modernising an old house, Nicola? Because that's what we're trying to do, Annabel and I. It's a big undertaking at any time, but when there's a date fixed for the work to be completed—painting, terracing, the lot——'

'Don't ask me, I don't know a thing about it.' She managed a fairly real smile, but that was because he was gazing towards her with the deceptively warm look in his eyes and for a moment she forgot how he really felt about her. A new face, someone with whom to amuse himself for a time? Aloud she said, 'I've just been talking to John on the phone and he's coming to collect me almost right away. I'll just go and collect my things, and say goodbye to Molly.'

'You're not leaving us now, tonight?' Molly had come into the room, an expression of disappointment shadowing her round, pleasant face. Regret tinged her tone. 'It's been such a joy having you here to stay. I thought you'd be with us until the weekend. Couldn't you possibly——'

'I'm sorry,' Nicola's voice came muffled, 'but something's come up, a bit of information about my uncle.' One thing about Uncle Walter, she thought wildly, he did come in useful at times as an excuse.

The words acted like magic, for Molly's face cleared instantly. 'Oh, that's different. For a moment I had this dreadful feeling that maybe you weren't happy here with us, that we'd done something ...' Her voice faltered into an embarrassed silence.

Nicola was acutely aware of Keith's watchful glance. At the same time she was aware that Annabel had raised her eyes from the architect's drawings, her expression one of mild interest. Why should Annabel care that she was leaving Sky Lodge? Secure in Keith's love, already planning their home together, what did it matter to Annabel that a strange girl who had come to stay here for a brief time, was now leaving for ever? Aloud she said, 'No, no, how could you imagine such a thing? You've been so good to me, all of you.'

'A bit of a sudden decision, isn't it?' Could it be a trick of the lamplight that made Keith's face seem to harden? 'I had the idea you weren't taking off from here until tomorrow?'

'I was, but——' She must avoid meeting his glance, that

look that seemed to say, 'I want you to stay.' If only it were for real! She said quickly, nervously, 'It seems that something's come up about Uncle Walter. John's been in touch with some people he wants me to contact, a family by the name of Fletcher.' There was no need to explain that she wouldn't be seeing the family until the weekend. 'They live up the coast somewhere, John says.'

'I get it. Well,' his cool glance was disturbing, 'if that's the way you want it!'

It isn't! her heart cried in protest. It's just that I have to go before I lay up any deeper suffering for myself.

On another level of her mind she was aware of Annabel's glance moving from Keith's set dark face (hadn't anyone ever crossed his wishes before?) to Nicola's flushed cheeks. 'Oh, let her go, Keith,' Annabel's tone was careless, 'if that's what she wants. You can't kidnap the girl, even if you wanted to.' To Nicola, the other girl's voice rang with the careless confidence of a girl so secure in Keith's love and affection that the possibility of his being attracted to anyone else simply wouldn't enter her mind. 'Anyone can see she's dying to get away.' She rose to her feet, stretching her arms lazily. 'I'll go and look up the rest of the plans. There's one I want your opinion on before we give the builder the final go-ahead.' She followed Molly out of the room.

Keith said quietly, 'Is that really the way you want it?'

Nicola couldn't sustain his deep intent look and turned her face aside, blinking away a mist of tears in her eyes. 'You've been so good, one way and another.' A picture flashed on the mental screen of her mind, of a man carrying a girl to safety up a cliff face. She gave an unsteady smile. 'Taking me in, looking after me. I don't know how to thank you.'

'Don't you?' In a few strides he was at her side. 'How about a goodbye kiss?' The next moment his seeking lips found hers in a kiss that sent everything else in her mind flying into oblivion. There was only ecstasy as her lips clung to his. The moment was shattered by Annabel's voice as she came along the hall. 'I've found it!' Abruptly Keith released her and when the other girl entered the room he was standing at the window, gazing out into the darkness. Nicola dropped down to a window seat in the shadows, hoping the other girl's penetrating glance wouldn't take in something daylight would have shown her in a moment. The flushed and tremulous face of a girl who had just been kissed!

CHAPTER SIX

JOHN arrived promptly on time to escort her to his home, and as the car swung around in the driveway she lifted a hand in response to Molly's vigorous wave. Keith and Annabel were waving too, but with them Nicola knew it was a mere gesture. It was almost a relief when a curve in the winding driveway hid the group from sight.

Over the ache in her heart she tried to concentrate on what John was saying. 'The Fletchers out at the coast, hope they can have something definite to pass on when they see you at the weekend.'

They sped around the dark curves of the roadway and once again she was conscious of the tang of pines all around them. Presently they were out on the highway with its borders of towering Phoenix palms, then they were running through suburban streets with lighted windows. All at once she recognised the house where she had spent her first night in the town, the orchard misty in the moon-glow. John was turning into the entrance when she caught a brief glimpse of a feminine figure amongst the shadows of spreading trees rising high above. Something about the slight form seemed vaguely familiar. The next moment the girl stepped forward and in the gleam of an overhead lamp Sharon's face, pale in the gloom, stared back at her.

'Wasn't that Sharon, standing in the shadows at the entrance?' she asked John, as they sped up the driveway.

'Sharon?' His tone was incredulous. 'I didn't see any-one!' But he had braked to a sudden stop and was back-ing the car along the way they had come. At the entrance gate he stopped with a lurch and the next moment he was out of the vehicle and peering along the empty street.

'You must have been mistaken,' he climbed back into the car and put a hand to the starter. 'There's no one about, and anyway, it couldn't have been Sharon. She's taken a job in another town, or so I've heard.'

'Maybe.' But Nicola knew there had been no mistake. She recalled the other girl's pale, accusing face. If Sharon only knew, she had no need to fear her influence with the man with whom she was obviously still deeply in love, despite the broken engagement.

'It's impossible,' John said tightly as they moved along the driveway once again. 'She wouldn't be hanging around here.'

Nicola made no answer. She knew she had not been in error.

The warm welcome extended to her by John's parents cheered her drooping spirits, for it seemed that the Hazletts were determined to make up to her for the unfortunate accident that had ended in her leaving them to stay with strangers. 'To think that it was our dog that caused all the trouble,' Mrs Hazlett mourned, her quick bright glance taking in Nicola's wan face. 'We'll never forgive our-selves ... you still look very pale.'

John's father came to seat himself at her side in the comfort of the lounge room, 'So long as you've recovered, lass. I posted off a letter to England today. I can tell you I've had a devil of a job trying to explain to your boss what's been happening to you since you called in to see us.'

Nicola twinkled up into the lined, friendly face. 'Don't worry. I don't think he'll be all that worried about me.'

'We were.' John had moved to the stereo. 'What would you like, Nicola? Jazz, folk music, rock, classics—we've got the lot.'

'I don't mind.' Suddenly she was desperately sorry she

had left Keith's house. It was crazy, it was beyond all reason, but she wished herself back in Sky Lodge. And all because she was missing the sight of a dark masculine face with an enigmatic expression. (Or was that only when he looked in her direction?)

'If you don't mind,' she murmured lamely, 'I think I'll have an early night.'

Immediately they were all fussing over her, Mrs Hazlett offering to see her to her room, her husband looking at her with almost fatherly concern, John jumping to pick up her suitcase. They were all so kind, why couldn't she be a little more sociable? It was no use; all she wanted was to be alone with her thoughts.

Mrs Hazlett paused in the doorway of the attractive bedroom with its pink floral wallpaper design of trailing rosebuds, and white-carpeted floor. 'I'll say goodnight, my dear, don't hurry out in the morning, have a sleep in, it will do you good.'

'I might do that.'

'Oh, just a thought.' Mrs Hazlett's shrewd gaze was fixed on Nicola's face. 'You didn't happen to notice a girl in a dark pants suit standing around by the gates as you came in tonight?'

Nicola raised her heavy glance. 'There was someone there. I thought it was Sharon, but John said that wouldn't be possible, that she had left Waihi to work in another town. When he went to look around there was no one there.'

'He doesn't know she's back, then?' Even in her turmoil of spirit Nicola was aware of an odd expression of triumph in the eyes of the older woman.

A little later she was transferring folded shorts and tops from her suitcase to a bureau drawer when snatches of conversation reached her through the open door. Mrs Hazlett was obviously speaking with a friend on the telephone in the hall. Her voice, shrill and penetrating, reached Nicola clearly. 'She was here again tonight, looking for John, but I was ready for her. I told her John was out with the English girl and that did it—worked like a charm!

I can tell you one thing though, Jean, this one is going to be harder to get rid of than the other one. She's not the girl for him, and he'll thank me for saving him from Sharon later on.'

Nicola's hand stilled and she stared absently down at the pile of clothing in her hand. Poor Sharon! If that was the effect that unrequited love had on a girl, leaving her with a longing so intense to see the loved one that nothing else mattered, not pride or self-esteem, she was glad she had made the break in time. Is that what you call it, jeered the small voice deep in her mind; I'd term it running away!

The next few days, as she waited for John to take her to the house at the coast, dragged interminably. The Hazletts did their best to make her feel welcome, but she couldn't seem to throw off the sense of restlessness and let-down that had been with her ever since leaving Sky Lodge. Never before had the hours dragged by so slowly as they did now. The two men in the family were away at the office all day and Mrs Hazlett, busily involved with her clubs and meetings, had apparently forgotten her promise to supply genealogy information to Nicola. In an effort to deaden the ache that niggled at her heart, she spent the hours exploring suburban streets with their neatly-tended homes and masses of flowering shrubs and plants, while Ben frisked along at her side. Sometimes she wandered down the main street of the town to gaze in display windows. The centenary celebrations had come to an end and coloured banners no longer fluttered overhead.

The evenings she found were easier to get through than the days. With John home from the law office, music flooded from the stereo. Sometimes they danced to pop melodies, or sat listening to records.

John's father never tired of plying her with questions about the village on the other side of the world where he had spent his childhood. Was the pub on the main street just the same? Had she walked on the common, picked blackberries along the roadside? She dredged her mind for details of the small town she had left behind.

One morning, hearing the postman's whistle, she went to the box at the gate to find, to her delight, a thin blue aerogramme addressed to herself. Bless you, Aunt! Nicola had written to her aunt shortly after her arrival telling her about the Waihi centenary. 'Wasn't I lucky to arrive here just at the right time! Not so lucky about finding any trace of Uncle Walter, though, but I'm busy making enquiries around the district.' There had been no need to worry Aunt Bella concerning her stupid accident that had resulted in her brief stay at Sky Lodge.

Nicola hadn't expected to receive mail quite so soon, but evidently her aunt hadn't waited for a letter from New Zealand before writing. Nicola was so excited she almost failed to notice the two other letters in the box. Both of the pale pink envelopes were addressed in neat feminine handwriting to Mr John Hazlett, and bore a row of tiny kisses on the back flap.

That evening when John returned home from the office, Nicola was in the lounge room with Mrs Hazlett.

'Hi, Mum! How are things, Nicola?' John greeted them. 'Any mail for me today?'

'There was for me,' Nicola said, 'a letter from home with all the latest gossip.'

'Great.' He spoke absently, his anxious gaze rolling over the mantelshelf. 'You're quite sure there was nothing for me?'

'Yes, there was!' Nicola spoke involuntarily. 'I brought it in with my aerogramme. Two letters ...' Her voice trailed away as she became aware of Mrs Hazlett's repressive frown.

'Oh no, my dear, you're mistaken. Those letters were for me. It's so easy to make a mistake, with my name being Jane. It can look so much like John that sometimes I'm not quite sure myself who a letter is addressed to. You can see for yourself, John,' she smiled towards her son, 'you know I always put any mail for you on the mantelshelf.'

Always? Nicola made the query silently. The pink envelopes had been addressed quite clearly to John, she was certain on that point, but she decided not to pursue the matter.

On the following day she strolled into town in search of postcards depicting local scenes that she would send to the office staff and to friends back home. Her selection was soon completed and she decided to return to the house and get the cards ready for mailing. Why fool herself? Why not admit that in spite of everything, deep inside her was a crazy hope that Keith would get in touch with her? She could force herself out of sight and hearing of him— but how to get the better of the longing?

As the days passed, however, she ceased to hope at each peal of the phone and when the ring did come it took her by surprise. John who had answered the call, came to her side. 'For you, Nicola. Keith wants a word with you!'

'Keith!' A wild excitement out of all proportion to the cause made her hurry down the passage.

She picked up the receiver. 'Hello?'

'Nicola!' The deep masculine tones held a warmth that was almost caressing, she thought, but of course that was absurd. 'How are you?'

'I'm fine! Just fine!'

'That's great! Molly's been on at me to find out how you are!' Molly! Her high spirits did a nose dive. 'She's just about dying of curiosity to know how you got on with the latest development in the Uncle Walter project?'

'Oh, that,' just in time she remembered she had used the matter of the impending visit to the Fletchers as a reason for her abrupt departure from Sky Lodge. 'Something came up,' would he catch the betraying nervousness in her tone, 'and they couldn't see me until the weekend. Seems they live right on the beach and have heaps of visitors.'

'Funny thing,' came the drawling masculine voice, 'I'm going up that way myself tomorrow to take a look at a stand of timber that's next on my list for cutting. I'll be going right past the beach.' Without waiting for an answer he ran on, 'Pick you up at nine.'

Her heart was beating fast. 'It might not suit them to

see me until the weekend.'

'No problem. They live there all the year round, I believe. It'll suit them fine, take my word for it. But if it makes you feel any happier, I'll give them a ring and tell them to expect you tomorrow.'

She heard her own voice saying weakly, 'John was going to take me at the weekend.'

His low chuckle did nothing to calm her tumultuous senses. 'That's what he thinks! See you tomorrow—and, Nicola——'

'Yes?'

'Don't forget to bring your swimsuit! 'Bye now!'

'Goodbye!' Suddenly she was feeling wildly, unaccountably happy. She couldn't help it. She had done her best to avoid seeing him, but if fate insisted on throwing them together it wasn't her fault, she argued with herself.

When she returned to the lounge John glanced up idly from the law journal he was reading. 'What did he want?'

She dropped to the floor, hands clasped around her knees, her eyes dreamy. 'Just something he wanted to tell me.' She forced her voice to a careless note. 'He has to make a trip up the coast tomorrow, he's going right past the Fletchers' place, he says, and he's offered to take me for the day—if they don't mind, of course.'

'They won't care which day you arrive there.' John looked disappointed. 'They told me they'd be home every day of the week, what with relations and kids all staying at the beach for the holidays. Any day would suit them. It's just—well, I thought it was a date we had, going up there.'

Nicola had a ridiculous thought that his voice held the peevish ring of a child being denied a special treat. She was aware too of Mrs Hazlett's quick suspicious glance darting from John to herself. It was a glance that changed to relief as Nicola said lightly, 'I know, I know—I'm sorry, but,' she sought wildly in her mind for a convincing excuse, 'I would like to go tomorrow. I'm so tired of waiting and this is the only clue that's turned up, thanks to you. Can't wait another day to find out!'

His face fell. 'Well, I guess that's it. I can't possibly get away tomorrow, not with the case I'm on coming up in court in the morning.'

In an effort to lighten his mood she said brightly, 'Tell me, what did you tell the Fletchers about me when you spoke to them on the phone about the advertisement?'

He shrugged. 'Just that you'd come out from England specially to trace a long-lost relative. All they really know about you is your name.'

'Well, that's a start!' Suddenly she was feeling light-hearted. 'And if it did happen to be Uncle Walter——'

John was eyeing her with his considering expression. 'If it were, if you got all that settled, would you take off back to England right away?' The question seemed to hang in the silence and Nicola was aware of Mrs Hazlett's glance darting from her son's downcast face to Nicola's flushed cheeks.

'No, no, I wouldn't do that, not with so much still left of my holiday time!'

A loud voice in her mind was beating out the unspoken thought. Not while Keith is still single—and here!

Because she suspected that today John's face would be set and disapproving, she delayed her arrival at the breakfast table until the men had left for their work at the office. She reflected that it wouldn't do him any harm not to have his own way for once. It was too bad that he allowed an adoring mother to manipulte his life. Why, she wondered, didn't Sharon just put John out of her mind and forget him? *Look who's talking*, came the jeering voice in her mind. If you had a vestige of common sense you'd forget Keith. Involuntarily she sighed. If only she could!

Immediately her crazy thoughts lifted on a wave of happiness. But I'm seeing him soon, so soon, she told herself, even if the meeting means nothing to him, no more than giving someone a lift to their destination. Only a stupid idiot like you would read anything personal into the offer. Of course it has nothing to do with me, but all the same ... She tucked the brand new black bikini into a roomy drawstring bag, threw in a towel, sunglasses, skin-lotion.

She was feeling so excited she couldn't eat any break-fast but the others had left the house, so there was no one to notice. Come to think of it, she had scarcely spoken to Mrs Hazlett since yesterday's evening meal. Could it be the older woman was avoiding her because of the letters which she had undoubtedly withheld from her son, no doubt telling herself it was all for his own good? For a moment Nicola considered speaking to John on the matter, then she decided it would be foolish to complicate things further, and besides, today was one of those golden days. A sky of such translucent blue it was almost touchable, an errant breeze to cool the air ... and Keith. Keith would be on his way. She gulped down a cup of coffee a moment before the ring of the doorbell sent Mrs Hazlett hurrying along the passage. In spite of all her resolutions that she wouldn't allow him to rattle her, just the sound of the deep masculine tones sent her good intentions into a riot of confusion.

'I've called for Nicola. We've got a date today. I'm giving her a lift along the road to the coast.' Such ordinary words. Nothing there surely to make her heart behave in this ridiculous way.

She hurried to the door. 'Here I am! All ready and on time!'

'Good for you!' The way in which he was regarding her, the expression in his dark eyes, was causing her to lose any shred of common sense she had left.

'Goodbye.' She was only half aware of Mrs Hazlett's faintly relieved tones. 'Have a good day, and I hope you get what you want today.'

'Thank you.' What she wanted? She crushed down the shaft of bittersweet longing that pierced her.

She became aware that Mrs Hazlett was regarding her with her shrewd bright gaze. 'At the Fletcher place, I mean.'

'Yes, I know.' With an effort she recovered her com-posure. 'I hope so too!'

'Expect us back when you see us!' Keith called gaily, and together they stepped out into the sunshine, moving towards a car standing in the driveway that she had last seen in the garages at Sky Lodge.

Nicola twinkled up at him. 'I thought you were going to see about milling some timber today?'

'That's right.' His glance tangled with hers and sent her spirits soaring. 'But I'm only giving the trees a look over. I won't be doing any cutting today.' He flung open the passenger door and saw her seated in the late-model, dust-coated car. 'Much more comfortable for the passenger this way than travelling in the Land Rover.'

'I wouldn't have minded.' *I wouldn't mind anything if I could just be with you.*

For a long moment the deep soft glance held her gaze. 'I don't believe you would.'

Soon they were turning in the wide driveway, moving up the pathway and out into the quiet street with its overhanging trees and wide, blossom-studded lawns surrounding timber homes.

'I've been doing some detective work since you left Sky Lodge,' he told her.

She glanced up at him, wide-eyed. 'Not Uncle Walter? You haven't found out anything?

Keith shook his dark head, his eyes fixed on the road junction ahead. 'Nothing new. No, it's the Fletcher crowd up the coast I wanted to get a line on if I'm to deliver you safely. Seems they live right over the beach, so they shouldn't be hard to find. Tell me, young Nicola,' did she imagine the caressing note in his voice? 'just say you did find out what you're wanting to know about the old boy, what then? Would it mean you'd go beetling off back to England by the next plane?'

She laughed lightly. It was so easy to laugh this morning. So difficult, her conscience reminded her, to remember Annabel. Aloud she answered, 'Funny you should say that. You're the second person who's asked me that question in the last day or two.'

'Am I now?' The husky tones were curiously low. 'Who was it? John?'

'As a matter of fact it was.'

To her surprise he was looking more than displeased, his mouth set and taut, his eyes staring straight ahead. Why did he look so put out? she wondered.

He said curtly, 'And you told him?'

'I said I'd stay until my return air ticket runs out.' Because of her conscience she added, 'I mean, it would be madness to waste the little time I have left, after my aunt has paid all the money for my fare out here.'

'But you'll be leaving here before long, taking a tour around the country?' His tone was harsh and demanding. She couldn't understand him at all. Leaving here! Leaving you, Keith! If he only knew. Aloud she managed a careless answer. 'I suppose so, but only if I find out the truth about Uncle Walter. The way things are going up to now, I'm beginning to wonder if I ever will!'

Keith was silent for a moment. When he spoke again his tone was flat, almost deadpan. 'Have you ever thought that it might be better all round, especially for your aunt in England, if you didn't discover what's happened to that missing relative of yours?'

'Better?' She turned puzzled eyes in his direction. 'What do you mean?'

He shrugged broad shoulders. 'There are lots of reasons that might cause a man to cut himself off from his family on the other side of the world.'

'Such as?'

'Who knows? It's on the cards he could have been in some sort of trouble with the police. Anything could have happened. Sometimes a man would prefer to drop out of sight rather than give relatives a shock, or risk losing their good opinion of him. Believe me, it happens.'

'Not with Uncle Walter! He——' She broke off, remembering this wasn't the first time that Keith had spoken to her in this vein. 'I told you before, he would never have done anything to be ashamed of!'

'How can you tell?' he asked calmly.

'I just ... know,' she said lamely.

The words fell into a silence. Then, 'Just thought I'd better give you a word of warning,' all at once he was lighthearted again, flashing a smile towards her, 'but I can see you're determined to get to the bottom of your mystery man!'

'That's right, and I don't care what I find out, so long as I find out something!'

Nicola relaxed against the seat, staring out of the window at the green paddocks with their grazing sheep and cattle. Quite suddenly the farmlands were left behind as they swung into a road winding down into the depths of a hill densely covered in native bush. Soon the thickly growing greenery shut out the sunlight and the pathway ahead vanished around a tree-lined bend. Then they were running down to sea level, looking out towards grassy slopes that had once been sandhills, sweeping past a rainbow of coloured baches built facing a calm blue sea.

Nicola was intrigued by the glittering sheet of blue outspread before her. 'Is this where we swim?'

'Not here. There are some super surf beaches further up the coast.'

She smiled up at him. 'I can hardly wait!'

Presently they had left the vistas of the ocean behind and were following a road bordered on either side with cleared farmlands. Nicola took in the boundaries of tall macrocarpa pines and the farm houses with their shelterbelts of leafy trees, perched on hilltops. 'The first swim of the season should be on a day like this,' Keith told her, speeding down a slope to come in sight of a sea that danced and sparkled with a myriad facets of sunlight.

She asked, 'Is this the swimming beach?'

'The coast is all great for swimming, but if you want to try the surf——'

'Oh, I do! I do!' Her face was alive with enthusiasm.

They came on it suddenly and Nicola drew in a breath of sheer delight, for below the roadway an expanse of golden sand stretched away into the misty distance. Keith braked to a stop and she watched a great comber surge in

to shore to splinter in a shower of foam, dragging wet
sand as it ebbed away. The waves were endless, a succession of white combers surging and breaking on a golden
shore. The dull roar of the surf was in her ears and on
her face she could feel the damp touch of blowing surf-
spray.

'It's so beautiful,' she breathed.

'Beats all the sheltered bays we've passed by, would
you say?'

'I can't wait to dive in!' Her hand was on the handle
of the car door, but he laid a detaining hand on her arm
and once again she felt a leap of her pulses at his
touch. 'Wait a minute! Tell me something, Nicola, how do
you rate as a swimmer?'

'Me? I can swim, if that's what you're getting at.'

'Not quite.' His tone was suddenly serious. 'It's a bois-
terous surf out there. Just stay close to me, then I'll
know you're all right. You'll be safe with me.'

Safe with him! If he only knew! Aloud she promised,
'Okay, I won't do anything stupid, if that's what you want.'

'That's the idea.' There was an enigmatic look in his
eyes. 'I'd hate to lose you now!'

Would you, Keith? Would you *really* care? But she
knew the answer to that query all too well.

He had turned to pick up his swimming trunks from the
back seat and soon they were making their way over the
sand towards a sandy bank where the roots of towering
pohutukawa trees snaked their precarious hold on the
crumbling slope. Keith's gaze went to a few scarlet tassels
gleaming amidst the thick greenery of the trees on the hillside. 'Looks like the Christmas trees are coming into bloom
early this year—that's a good sign.'

She said in a puzzled voice, 'A sign of what?'

'Aha, I'll have to let you into some of the native lore.
The Maoris have an old saying that the early blossoming
of the pohutukawa trees means the start of a long hot
summer.'

She stared up at him wide-eyed. 'You really believe
it?'

'Sure. You will too when you've lived here for a while.'

The shaft of pain came without warning. How strange that he should speak as if she would be here for ever instead of a two-month trip. If only ... determinedly she pushed the longing aside. Today she refused to allow anything to dim the happiness of her golden day, a day that had been handed to her by fate.

All at once she became aware of a teasing light in his eyes. 'Looking for changing sheds, madam? They're right here!'

'Oh! I see what you mean!' Swiftly she dropped down in the shelter of a great gnarled tree trunk. It was a matter of only a few minutes to slip out of her clothes. She placed them in a fork of the tree, out of reach, she hoped, of tossing spray. Swift though she had been in changing into her bikini, she found Keith waiting for her down on the wet sand. Could this be love, this stupid hopeless feeling she had for him? Made him seem to her so heartbreakingly attractive? Muscular, slim-hipped, sun-bronzed to the waist of his swimming trunks, he wore the smile he seemed to keep specially for her.

He took her hand in his and together they plunged into the foaming surf. The next moment a great comber surged towards them, catching Nicola off balance, and she found herself plunging down, down into swirling green depths. But a strong hand wrenched her to the surface and, gasping and laughing, she dashed sea water from her eyes and flung the streaming hair back from her wet forehead.

'Look out!' Another breaker was sweeping towards them. 'Dive through it!' Keith called, and they emerged a moment later to swim out beyond the crash and thunder of breaking surf. Again and again they returned to wait for the approach of a white-capped comber, to drop down and be carried swiftly into a welter of foam and the firm sand underfoot. For Nicola time ceased to exist and there was only the tossing waves where she and Keith were in a magic, invigorating world of their own.

In a pause between oncoming breakers Nicola was treading water. 'How about a race? But you'll need to give me a good start. I'm no match for your butterfly stroke!'

'Right! You start—now!'

Laughing, she began to make her way amongst the surging waves, realising idly that the tide had turned. Ahead of her she glimpsed a patch of calm water amidst boiling surf and she struck out towards it. Once she imagined she heard Keith calling to her and she increased her pace. The next moment she reached the oddly calm water. At the same moment she became aware of a strong rip of the tide and attempted vainly to fight against it. Then without warning a powerful wall of water was swirling her around, and helplessly she felt herself being swept out to sea. The thought darted through her mind that she must go with the tide and later try to make her way back. All at once the shore looked a long distance away and a terrible tiredness was weighing her down. She felt almost too exhausted to go on and she knew there was no possibility of turning, then strong arms were beneath her shoulders. 'Just relax, take it easy.' Keith took her towards the shore and by the time they reached the shallows she had all but recovered herself, though she could still feel the stupid leaden sensation in her limbs.

'I'm all right now.' She made to put her feet down on firm sand, but he caught her up in his arms and strode through the foaming waves.

He was still holding her when they reached the dry sand with its straggling marram grass. 'I must have been crazy, to let you get away from me like that, with a rip tide and a patch of white water right ahead of you.'

'It was my idea,' she said shakily.

'I blame myself. If anything had happened to you, Nicola, to you——' His eyes were dark and intent and she saw with a little shock of surprise that his face had paled beneath the tan.

'Well, it didn't—thanks to you!' She made no attempt to struggle, she didn't want to. She hoped he would put it down to weakness that she made no attempt to drop to the warm sand.

'Forgive me, for not taking better care of you.' As his

mouth came down on hers she felt the taste of salt water on his lips, then there was only ecstasy. It was only afterwards that sanity returned with a rush. It was merely reaction on his part, he really seemed to imagine she might have drowned out there in the lonely sea. She shivered and, gently, he put her down.

'You're cold. I should have thought of chill and shock. Get your things on right away, while I make up a fire.'

Nicola didn't really feel all that bad, but now that common sense had reared its ugly head, she didn't dispute the matter.

The stupid shaking seemed to make the matter of getting dressed a slow process, but at last she came back from the shelter of the pohutukawa tree to join him. She dropped to the sand, wringing out the long dripping mane of her hair, then sat, hands linked around her knees, watching him arrange driftwood lattice-fashion in a sheltered spot on the sand. Once again the sense of dreamy content took over. 'You saved my life,' she said suddenly.

Keith was kneeling, putting a match to the pile of sticks. 'You'd have made it back to the shore all right, given time.'

But Nicola knew that for her time had been running out and without his help she would have had no chance of survival. 'No, I wouldn't. That's not true, you know——'

'Have it your own way! Pity we didn't happen to be Chinese folk living a long while ago.'

'*Chinese?*'

'That's right.' His eyes were on the flickering flame. 'Seems they had a quaint idea over in their country that anyone who rescues a person from dying more or less owns that person for the rest of their life. It would mean that you would belong to me—for always.' His eyes were alight as he looked her full in the face. 'How does that strike you?'

It struck her as perfectly heavenly, but, confused, she looked away from his brilliant gaze and began to pile sand over her bare feet. 'It could be awkward,' she commented.

'It could be wonderful.'

She went on covering her feet with fine golden sand, afraid he might glimpse the longing in her eyes.

At that moment the spell was shattered as an old car sped into sight along the sandy road, to lurch to a stop on the grassy bank above them.

Nicola forced her voice to a careless note. 'We've got company.'

'Worse luck!' It was difficult to resist him when he grinned at her in that intimate way. 'Trouble is, it was just too good to last.'

Secretly Nicola couldn't have agreed with him more, even though she told herself it was just as well the interruption had come when it did.

The party of young people were a friendly, noisy gang, who were evidently acquainted with Keith, 'You didn't think you were going to keep the whole beach to yourself?' A picnic party of two girls and two young men scrambled down the bank to join them. One of the girls was eyeing Nicola curiously. 'Where's Annabel today?' she asked Keith.

He seemed to Nicola to be unperturbed by the question.

'She's working flatout on her Gown of the Year entry If she doesn't carry off the trophy it won't be for want of trying!'

Nicola was only vaguely aware of the talk and laughter echoing around her. 'Where's Annabel?' It was, she reminded herself, the normal reaction at the sight of Keith being accompanied by any other girl. How many more times did she need to have it pinpointed that the other two were a team, a man and woman team?

With an effort she wrenched her mind back to the present, realised the girls were inviting her and Keith to join them in a friendly cuppa. Already one of the men had gone to the car and was holding in his hand a blackened billy. Keith declined the offer and presently, to the echoes of loudly-called 'goodbyes' and 'you'll be sorry!' they were in the car and heading for a sandy slope ahead.

Nicola watched Keith's well-shaped, tanned hand on the

wheel as they sped on, the sea breeze tossing her damp hair around her face. A strand blew across his eyes and roughly she jerked it free, evading the arm he had thrown across her shoulders and moving as far away from him as possible. The sense of physical relaxation lent by sea and sun was still with her, but the wild excitement of the day had fled. An extra girl, was that the way he thought about her? A quiet girl in contrast to Annabel's endless chatter and light laughter? Was that what he wanted? She saw the green farmlands with patches of bush running up the gullies between hills, through a haze of pain. Nevertheless, pride helped her to hide the heart-ache and as he told her the names of the bays they were passing and pointed out farmhouses on the hills, she contrived to make a show of interest and to supply the right answers to his impersonal questions—at least she hoped so. If the lighthearted gaiety of the morning for him, too, had fled, it was his own fault, she thought hotly. At this moment she almost hated him, and hating him somehow made it easier to blink away the unshed tears.

All at once she realised they were running through a street of brightly painted timber houses and soon they were passing through an area lined with stores, restaurants and sports grounds.

'It's quite a township, especially in the summer,' Keith told her in his new impersonal tone. She stole a glance towards his closed face and decided she couldn't hate him, not for long. She loved him in spite of everything and she couldn't seem to help herself. For something to say she asked. 'The Fletchers live near the beach?'

'Bang on, actually, from what I've heard.' They swung into a quiet street overlooking an expanse of sandhills and blue sea. 'Pick out the best house in the street.'

She leaned forward, her gaze fixed on a low, ranch-style home built of creamy-coloured bricks, with a blue-tiled roof. French doors were open on to a wide terrace where a group of people were seated on white wrought-iron seats. 'Not that gorgeous place we're coming to now?'

'That's the one they described to me when I rang to warn them we were on our way!' They turned into a wide driveway bordered with flowering plants and presently they took the steps leading to a side door. Keith's ring of door chimes brought to the door a pleasant-looking woman of middle age. Because of the new and attractive dwelling, Nicola had expected to find a more glamorous type of owner than the homely-looking person who was smiling towards her. There was a puzzled expression in Mrs Fletcher's eyes as her gaze went from Keith to Nicola.

'I think you're expecting me to turn up some time to-day,' Nicola said in her soft voice. 'In connection with the advertisement Mr Hazlett put in the paper?'

'Oh! *You* are Miss Ayres?' The stranger appeared quite bewildered, but the next moment she recovered herself. 'Come in, I'm so glad you've come. It was such a shock seeing you at the door,' her heightened colour gave her away. 'You see, from what Mr Hazlett told us on the phone, we expected to see someone of at least fifty-five.'

Nicola laughed! 'He would be talking about my aunt, I expect.' Briefly she introduced Keith.

'Mr Lorimer!' Mrs Fletcher's voice was warm and welcoming, 'Do come inside. There's a crowd of young people out on the terrace and you're bound to know some of them.'

'Thank you,' regretfully Keith declined the invitation, 'but I only stopped by to deliver Nicola. I'm a timber man and I'm due up in Golden Valley to have a look at a stand of timber I promised to cut.'

'I'm so sorry you can't stay.'

As her hostess drew her inside the house, Nicola found herself immediately surrounded by a throng of people. Everyone talked at once and it was quite a time before the older woman could draw her aside.

'Come along, my dear. You must be longing to discover if your Uncle Walter is our one too.' Mrs Fletcher's good-natured face crinkled in a wide smile. 'Imagine, you might be our long-lost cousin all the way from England!'

She led the way to a study off the hall and handed Nicola a letter, but as Nicola's gaze swept the faded back-handed script her brief hopes of coming to an end of her search died away. 'The handwriting is quite different from that of the postcard I have,' she said regretfully. She studied the sepia photograph the older woman was handing to her. 'No, there's just no resemblance.'

'What a pity! You must feel so disappointed about this.'

Nicola slipped on another bright smile; it was getting to be a habit lately. 'Oh, I'm not giving up yet. It's just that it's so much harder than I expected, tracing someone you know so little about——'

'Hey, Mum——' The door was flung open and Nicola found herself gazing up, up, into the bronzed face of a blond young giant who had stopped in his tracks, an incredulous expression in his vividly blue eyes.

'My son Wayne,' said Mrs Fletcher. A mischievous light twinkled in her eyes. 'Wayne, this is Miss Ayres.'

His mouth dropped open in astonishment. 'Are *you* Miss Ayres?' At last he got the words out. 'Why, what a surprise!'

Nicola looked back at him, mystified. Clad in dark shorts, he was bare to the waist, muscular chest and strong limbs sun-darkened to a deep mahogany tan. 'What did you expect Miss Ayres to be like, for heaven's sake?'

'Not you, especially not a girl like you.' Nicola was feeling slightly embarrassed beneath his openly appreciative gaze.

The small girl whom Nicola had all but tripped over in the hall had wandered into the room and now raised a bright impudent face from the apple she was muching. 'You said Miss Ayres would be a maiden lady, all dressed up with white gloves and a funny flower hat.' She had a clear, carrying voice, 'What's a maiden lady, Grandma?'

Wayne flung a hand over the small mouth. 'Shut up, you little horror!'

'You said,' shrieked the child, escaping his hold, 'she'd be a fuddy-duddy old thing who'd bore everyone to death.

You said——' the last words were drowned as Wayne swept the child up in his arms, bundled her out of the room, and closed the door.

His mother was laughing. 'Serves you right for jumping to conclusions!'

'Just a perfectly natural mistake.' Clearly, Nicola thought, Wayne was trying to bluff his way out of a difficult situation. 'Miss Ayres won't hold it against me, I know.'

She met his disarming grin with a smile. 'I'll think about it.'

'I'll make it up to you,' he promised. 'I'll take you swimming, sunbathing, surfing—anything you say. You can even come with me and take a look around the club-house if you like?'

She said bewilderedly, 'The clubhouse?'

'He's a member of the local surf life-saving team,' his mother explained. 'You know, those gorgeous big hunks of manhood you see pictures of, all tanned and muscular, who go striding along the beach and manning surf boats.'

'Not to mention saving the odd life,' Wayne put in.

'True, true, they do a good job.' Mrs Fletcher turned to Nicola. 'You should go along with him, Miss Ayres. It's quite interesting to see the way in which everything along the shore is geared to getting a rescue organised without a moment's delay.'

'I'd like to,' said Nicola, and meant it.

'Right! It's a date!' His glance moved to the photograph on the shelf nearby. 'How did it go, the genealogy bit? Okay, I hope?' His gaze lingered on her face. 'We could do with someone like you in the family.'

She shook her head. 'Sorry, but it didn't work out. I just get a lead of some sort, then it peters out. I've only got a few weeks left before my air ticket runs out, so for me it's a sort of race with time.'

'Think of it as your Kiwi holiday,' Wayne told her. 'You did say,' he urged, 'that you'd like to see the clubhouse?'

'And the beach. You can't imagine how different it all is here, coming straight from winter into a kind of instant

summer.' She pulled a mocking face. 'And a real lifeguard
and all!' Somehow she was feeling very much at home
with this smiling young giant and the kindly woman
who was his mother.

CHAPTER SEVEN

NICOLA was only too glad to go with Wayne. Today she
was grateful for any diversion that would serve to take her
mind from Keith—and Annabel.

He led the way down an indoor staircase and out to the
roadway below, then they were taking a sandy track down
to the beach. Plodding over great drifts of sand, they made
their way in the direction of the high timber building
with its look-out tower built on the beach. Below the surf
clubhouse she glimpsed a stack of surf-skis and a surf-
boat.

On an expanse of smooth sand now, she hurried along
at the side of the barefooted bronzed giant. 'Have you
rescued many swimmers from the surf—your club, I
mean?'

'Have we ever?' Even as he spoke his gaze raked the
sea where swimmers were disporting themselves in an area
marked by red and yellow flags as a safe swimming area
where lifesavers were on duty. 'Just in the Auckland
district, surf lifesaving patrols bring in hundreds of folk
from boiling seas and rips.'

'They must be very grateful to you for rescuing them.'

He grinned. 'You must be joking! Most of them don't
even say, "thanks, mate." Too embarrassed, or suffering
from effects of shock maybe, or else they've got an idea
they didn't need rescuing in the first place. Mostly we
pull out idiots who've gone swimming in their jeans and
got caught in the rip at the far end of the beach.'

Nicola scarcely heard him. If only it hadn't been Keith
to whom she owed gratitude for a sea rescue! Come to

think of it, she owed him a great deal, one way and another.

Up in the look-out tower to the clubhouse, Nicola was entranced by the vista outspread below. The beautiful coastline with its islands, sheltered beaches and rolling surf. Nearby above the sheltered waters of a bay, bush-clad hills seemed to shimmer against a blue sky.

Wayne, however, was taking in Nicola's face, flushed to an apricot tint with the effects of sun and salt, dark hair blowing around her shoulders in the breeze. 'To think I almost didn't come home this afternoon! How lucky can you get?'

'Afraid of having to meet that boring old Miss Ayres?' she taxed him mischievously.

He held her smiling gaze. 'If I take you along the beach with me for a stroll, will you promise never to remind me of that again?'

'If you like.'

Soon they were making their way along the gleaming sand, the touch of surf-spray moist on their faces. Wayne eyed her consideringly. 'How about a swim?'

'Not with that horrible Miss Ayres you couldn't escape from?'

'You promised.' At his ferocious expression she ran along the water's edge with Wayne in swift pursuit. He caught up with her, quickly, but she tore herself free, laughing. 'My bikini, it's up at the house, though I'm so wet now that I may as well go in just as I am. But of cause I wouldn't,' she remembered she was in the company of a surf rescue member, 'not jeans in the surf!'

'I'll be right back!' He tossed a grin back to her over a bare bronzed shoulder.

Nicola strolled along the sand, stooping to gather up small golden translucent shells as she went on. They would be something to remind her of her New Zealand holiday, but deep down she knew that the fleeting days in these sun-splashed islands of the South Seas would be difficult to forget.

Presently she and Wayne were plunging into curling, white-crested breakers and afterwards they threw themselves down on the warm sand while the hot sunshine beat down on their backs.

'Here they come,' Wayne groaned, 'the family in full strength!'

As his mother and sisters and some small children came to join them Nicola was aware of a sense of satisfaction in being drawn into the happy atmosphere. And yet, she mused wistfully a little later, it was funny how even in the company of these warm-hearted people, with Wayne devoting himself to her comfort, time dragged. For her time had come to be measured by the hours she must wait until Keith arrived back from his trip to the bush to pick her up on the return journey.

'Mind if I ask you something?' The diffident tones of Wayne's young sister Jane roused her from her musing.

Nicola forced a smile. 'Ask away.'

'Was it really Keith Lorimer who brought you along here today?'

Nicola's heart gave a jerk, but she schooled her voice to a careless inflection. 'That's right. I had a stupid accident and he took me to his home until I got better.'

'You were staying at Sky Lodge, *with him*?' Jane's gaze was on Nicola's downcast face. 'I guess, being a stranger here, you wouldn't know that he happens to be the most exciting bachelor for miles around. Every girl in the place would just love to have a date with him,' she giggled, 'including me! Oh, I know everyone says he's madly in love with that Annabel girl, but he's not married to her yet—Mum,' her voice quickened and she swung around to face the older woman, 'I've just had a super idea. Would you do something for me?'

'That depends.' Mrs Fletcher's voice was wary.

'*Please*, Mum! It's about Keith Lorimer. You saw him today, he knows you. Could you ask him to my birthday party?'

Her mother's placid face was unperturbed. 'I could send him an invitation, but that isn't to say he'll come.'

'It won't do you any good, you know,' her older sister

pointed out unfeelingly. 'They say he never goes anywhere without his Annabel.'

Jane's young face fell, but she said stubbornly, 'He might.'

'Bet you my silver bracelet you're always giving hints about that he turns you down!'

Jane glared back at her sister. 'You'll be sorry you made that offer!'

Wayne asked lazily. 'What's so special about the guy, anyway?'

'Wait until you meet him,' his young sister breathed, 'just wait!'

'No need to do that,' Wayne told her, 'here he comes now.'

Nicola had already caught sight of the tall masculine figure who was striding over the sand towards the group.

'Hi, everyone!' His smile, that included the party, somehow lost itself in Nicola's direction. 'The house seemed to be deserted, but I thought I'd find you all down here.'

Mrs Fletcher attempted to make introductions, but in the sudden hubbub of shouting children and mothers enforcing silence, she gave up the attempt. She said in her kindly way, 'Why don't you join us?'

'Thanks, but I have to get back.'

'Oh, must you, so soon?' There was genuine disappointment in the chorus of voices.

'Afraid so.'

'Before you go, there's someone here who wants very much to meet you,' said Mrs Fletcher, conscious of a vigorous prodding at her side. 'This is my daughter Jane.'

'Nice to meet you, Jane,' said Keith in his easy way.

Now that she had got the opportunity she wanted, Jane seemed suddenly at a loss for words. It was her mother who said quietly, 'Pop in and see us any time you're out this way, Mr Lorimer. We keep open house here at the beach and there's usually someone at home.'

'That's kind of you. Right now though we've got to get cracking, if it's okay with you, Nicola?'

'Just a moment,' Mrs Fletcher said. 'Nicola dear, why

not come back and stay for a couple of weeks with us? After this weekend there'll be a room to spare. There's a cottage at the back of the house and we'd love to have you make use of it.

'Now that's an idea!' Wayne's voice rang with enthusiasm. 'Don't forget that you're a cousin of ours—well, sort of.'

'That's kind of you.' Nicola's thoughts were churning wildly. The invitation would take her away from the town where any day, any night, she might run into Keith, and that way danger lay. Here at the beach house with these friendly folk she could swim and take walks and maybe help a little with the children, be of some use and most important of all, make herself forget the man who stood waiting for her answer. That was all that mattered now, to make herself forget. It was an opportunity she couldn't afford to miss.

'I'd like to come,' she said quietly.

'That's settled, then,' Jane said happily. 'Get John to bring you along as soon as he can.'

The chorus of goodbyes followed them as Nicola and Keith turned away and made their way back to the beach house and the waiting car.

A little later, seated in the vehicle, she looked up at him, taking in the strong face and mobile mouth. What was it about him that held her so? Once again she felt a surge of dangerous content and vainly she tried to fix her mind on her surroundings as they sped through the clean wide streets where girls clad in swimsuits and sun-frocks and young men, bare to the waist and wearing gaudily patterned beach shorts. strolled amongst the modern stores.

When she told Keith of the failure of her mission, he flashed his devastating smile. 'Why not just call it a day? You've done just about all anyone could do, made all the enquiries possible around the district. Short of interviewing every Fletcher bod in the country, you've come to a full stop. You know something? You're wasting an awful lot of time searching when you could be out and about enjoying yourself. Ever heard how many folk there are in the country who just disappear without trace?'

'No.'

'I haven't either, but it must be one hell of a lot!'

It was safer, she decided, to keep to the subject of Uncle Walter. 'I can try one more thing,' she said.

All at once his tone sharpened. 'You don't mean you're leaving Waihi?'

'You asked me that once before.' As if it mattered to him whether or not she stayed, except as a sort of extra girl to keep on hand when he was in the mood for a little light lovemaking. Maybe he even felt a certain tendresse for her, having come to her rescue not once but on two occasions! Aloud she said, 'No, I haven't changed my mind about staying around here.' *How could I, knowing you were here?* 'My idea is to put an ad in one of the national newspapers. It might start something—if I'm lucky!'

'You could give it a go.'

She pouted. 'You don't seem very optimistic!'

'No harm in going ahead with it.' All at once his voice softened. 'You do *try*, don't you, Nicola?'

'It's what I'm here for,' she said with spirit, 'and don't forget that I'm the one who has to face my aunt when I get home. I've got to have a scrap of information to take back. If I could just find out something about him, it would make her happy.'

'You reckon?' His enigmatic tone puzzled her.

They left the township behind and now there was only the winding road ahead, cutting through sheep-dotted hills, with vistas of blue sea that were lost to view as they swung around the curves. Much later they sped down a slope and she realised they were passing the sheltered bay where she and Keith had paused on their journey to swim together. Could it have been only this morning?

As they went on to take a road winding through thickly growing bush on high hills, his arm was thrown carelessly around her shoulders and, weakly, she let it stay. Just his touch was sufficient to send her spirits soaring out of orbit. What harm could there be in the gesture? She let herself relax against him and once again enchantment took over. He was singing, his voice so low she barely caught the words. It was a song she had always loved, now it had for her a bittersweet significance. 'Release me, and let me love again.'

As they sped on, she caught glimpses of drifts of sand and the water beyond. She saw it all through a haze of deep content and was sorry, weak fool that she was, when they left the bush-clad hills behind and swept through familiar suburban streets. She roused herself as they neared her destination and when Keith braked to a stop on the wide driveway near the house, she had herself well in hand. Or so she had imagined. But now he was gazing at her in a speculative way. 'What would you say if I asked you to let me take you out tomorrow night?'

Annabel was away in town for a few days. The thought came unbidden and gave her sufficient strength of mind to make her voice cool and careless. 'I'd say, Sorry, Keith, but I've got an engagement tomorrow night.' Even to her own ears the words had a ring of untruth. She added wildly, 'With John.'

Something in his angry silence put her thoughts in a flurry. She heard herself add, 'It was good of you to take me with you today.'

'But you still won't let me take you out tomorrow?' His voice was cold steel. 'Is that it?'

She was silent, sick with misery. If only she didn't care so much she would have been able to handle the situation. She thought wildly, 'Now he hates me, and no wonder!'

'So long as we know where we stand. Let me know,' he gritted, 'when you can make up your mind what you do want.' The next moment he had swung around on his heel and getting into the car, roared away at speed.

Nicola stared after the fast disappearing car with eyes misted with unshed tears. You couldn't blame him for thinking she was the type of girl who took a delight in leading men on, one moment meeting his kiss with passion, why not admit it, then refusing to see him again. He *must* know the reason. How could he expect her to play second fiddle to the girl he planned to marry? How could he?

Oh, he made her so angry! At this moment she would have liked to hit him, hard! He deserved it, being so obtuse, pretending he had no idea of the reason why she couldn't allow herself to become too friendly with him. Couldn't— or didn't dare? Either way she had no choice in the matter. Her anger sustained her all the way back to the house.

John showed little surprise at her lack of success with her enquiries. He looked at her through the lenses of gold-rimmed glasses. 'At least you got something out of the trip.'

She pulled a face. 'I suppose you mean sunburn and red cheeks.'

He studied the apricot tan of her face. 'It suits you, does something for you, makes you look more like a Kiwi girl somehow.'

She laughed, and went on to tell him of her invitation to stay at the beach cottage.

'Great!' John looked elated. 'I could take some leave from the office, come over every day and see you—that is,' his tone was suddenly serious, 'if you wanted me to.'

'Sounds like fun. Come if you like.' The anger had died away leaving only a sense of loss and emptiness. But what else could she have done but send Keith away?

'Hello, Nicola,' John's mother had come to join the two young people, 'have a good day?' Mrs Hazlett spoke absently.

'I had a fantastic swim.'

As the older woman turned away John asked, 'Any phone calls for me today?' Nicola was aware of a note of tension beneath the commonplace words.

His mother paused in the doorway. 'Only one, from Sharon.'

'Sharon!' He spun around, his face alight with an inner excitement.

So he does care for her, Nicola reflected. He tries not to, but deep down his feeling for her is still there. You can't turn love off just like that, because you want to. A voice in her mind jeered, *'You should know!'*

'What did she want?' John's voice was terse. 'Is she back in Waihi now?'

Mrs Hazlett shrugged her shoulders. 'She didn't say. I told her you were tied up just now, with Nicola being here and all, and she rang off.'

'I get it.' John appeared to have recovered his poise. 'I guess, whatever it was she wanted, she'll ring again.' His tone lacked any particular feeling.

'You can say that again!' Mrs Hazlett slammed the door angrily as she left them.

John's mother's enthusiasm over Nicola's invitation to the beach house was so warm that Nicola couldn't help a sneaky thought that tilted her lips in amusement. Clearly Mrs Hazlett had yet to learn of her son's holiday plans that included most days spent on the beach a few miles distant, with Nicola.

'Have a good time,' she called, as John saw Nicola into the big red car standing in the driveway.

Presently they were out of town and passing vehicles towing trailer boats and caravans and battered-looking cars with twin fins of surfboards rising from the roof, driven by carefree-looking young men with deeply tanned faces and sun-bleached hair.

On her arrival at the beach house Nicola found her welcome to be as warm as before. Presently her hostess showed her to a comfortable two-roomed cottage at the back of the house. 'You'll have meals with us, of course,' Mrs Fletcher said in her motherly way. That night there was a barbecue meal outside, where Wayne and his father cooked steak, sausages and succulent lamb chops while the womenfolk set out bowls of salads, crusty bread and cold drinks.

Nicola gathered that the two married sisters, Ann and Merle, together with their young children, were staying at the beach house while their husbands sweated out the summer in city offices. The youngest daughter, Jane, came home for weekends from boarding school, but soon she too would be home for the holidays.

As for Wayne, he put himself out to take her sightseeing,

surfing or boating during his free time. Idly she wondered at the reactions of friends back home could they have met up with him—the sort of 'golden look' there was about him, his magnificent physique, tanned skin and sun-bleached blond hair. If only I could have fallen in love with him instead of with Keith, she thought. For something told her that he wouldn't need a great deal of encouragement to care for her, and to care quite a lot.

Gradually the sun-splashed days fell into a pattern. In the mornings while Wayne was on patrol duty at the club, Nicola took the young children down to the beach. In the afternoons Wayne would bring the runabout close inshore and Nicola would wade through the breakers. She enjoyed the moment when the engine roared into life and they shot over the waves to explore the endless bays and inlets.

Half way through the first week of her stay John telephoned.

'Just thought I'd give you a ring to see how you're getting along out there. Plenty of sun-tan?'

She laughed. 'You'll hardly know me next time you see me!'

'You reckon? I'll be able to judge that for myself pretty soon. I've arranged to take a few days off work next week. My trailer boat is moored out in the inlet, so we'll be able to get around the coast a bit. How does that strike you?'

'I can hardly wait. But I didn't even know you owned a boat. What do you call her?'

'The *Lady Sharon*.'

'Oh!' To fill the awkward pause she said quickly, 'I'll see you soon, then.'

Thoughtfully she laid the receiver back in its cradle. John must have cared for Sharon at one time, she mused, to name his boat after her.

CHAPTER EIGHT

WITHIN the space of a few days, it seemed to Nicola that Wayne was never far from her side. Indeed, he appeared to regard as wasted any of his free time spent away from her.

One day she chided him about it. 'You don't need to worry about keeping me amused.' They had been swimming and she was towelling dry her long dark hair while he lay beside her on the sand. 'Just being at the beach like this and strolling along in the sunshine, it's a complete change to me, coming from the English winter.'

'A worry, looking after you?' He had propped his face on his elbows, looking up at her, and at the expression in his eyes she glanced swiftly away. He was young and free and good to look at. The huskiness in his tone couldn't mean he was attracted to her so much, so soon—or could it? The last thing she desired was to light fires she had no hope of keeping alight. The next moment she told herself she was being stupidly imaginative. She was someone new in his life, that was all.

All at once his sun-browned hand covered her own. 'You do like being with me, though?'

She raised clear blue eyes. 'Oh, I do! It's all another world to me here——'

'I wasn't meaning the scenery.'

She said lightly, 'It wouldn't be much fun, swimming, sunbathing, boating, any of it, by myself.'

His eyes were half thoughtful, half quizzical. 'Sometimes I get the idea you're not really with me, that you're miles away. When you think no one's looking, you look so sad.'

'Me?' Hurriedly she pulled her features into a bright mask of gaiety. 'Why should I be sad? With all this ...' Her gaze travelled over the sea, shot with a myriad dancing sunbeams. I'm as happy as can be, especially here.'

'Especially with me?' he persisted.

She was letting the sand run through her fingers. 'Of course.' Her words seemed not to take the anxious expression from his blue eyes.

'Say it as if you mean it.'

'Of course I like being with you.' She tried to put a warm inflection into her tone.'

'I get it,' he said quietly. 'There's someone else, isn't there? A guy you're really interested in. Don't try to put me off,' he added quickly, 'it sticks out a mile.'

Nicola's face was aghast. What could she say? She had tried so hard to appear happy and carefree. She had been happy—well, part of the time. Only someone who cared enough about her to notice her unguarded expression could have guessed her secret.

The silence lengthened and at last she said lamely, 'If there is there's no future in it. He scarcely knows I exist.' (Except maybe as an extra girl to amuse him when he's in the mood for company and Annabel isn't around.)

'That guy over in England,' Wayne gritted out the words, 'must be out of his mind!'

Nicola let it go at that.

All at once his grim expression lightened. 'If that's the way it is with you, I'm not giving up hope. At least I've still got a chance. Tell me,' his voice dropped to an appealing note, 'I have, haven't I?'

'I'll tell you when,' she promised. 'Anyway,' she made an attempt to lighten his mood, 'with all the girls I've met at the dances in the clubhouse, and you beach patrol guys are rather eye-catching, you know——' It was no use, he wasn't even listening.

'Other girls aren't you. There's something about you, I can't explain. I don't want any other girl, just you.'

She tried to laugh away his serious mood. 'Summer madness?'

'Summer love. The sort that could last for ever.' He made to put his arms around her, but she jumped to her feet.

'I feel like another swim. Coming?'

'If you want to.'

Hand in hand, they ran into the breakers.

Wayne seemed to be her devoted slave and she wondered if he had been this way with other girls he had been friendly with in the past. It was Ann who answered the query for her. They were down on the sand, idly tossing a beach ball to the children playing around them, when Ann said lightly, 'You know something, Nicola, you've really made an impression on brother Wayne. I've never seen him treat a girl the way he does you. Anyone would think you were made of candyfloss and had to be protected even from the sea breeze, let alone any other guy who happens to be around. Did you notice the way he glowered at Bill yesterday, just because he stopped on the beach to talk? Anyone would think the fellow was making off with you!'

'I thought it was just his way!'

'Just his way!' Wayne's sisters joined in the laughter. 'You should have seen the way he acted with other girl-friends! Not that there've been many, only two actually. He treated them quite casually, as if they could look after themselves. No wonder they got sick of it. Then you come along and wow! What a difference!'

'All that after-shave,' laughed Merle.

'And the trouble he takes with his clothes,' chimed in Ann.

'You should hear him when he's with his mates. It's Nicola this and Nicola that. He thinks there's no one like you.'

'Just as well you're not staying in the country,' Ann's tone was thoughtful, 'or he might really go overboard for you. Unless there could be a happy ending, of course?'

You couldn't blame them, Nicola thought, for quizzing her in this way. Wayne was their only brother and they didn't want to see him hurt. But what could she do? She tossed back the red and white beach ball while she sought wildly in her mind for a reply. In the end all she came up with was, 'You're both imagining things. I mean, I've only been here a week, and lots of girls must fall for him. He's a nice boy.'

'It's who *he* falls for that matters,' Merle pointed out.

'I guess,' Nicola agreed on a sigh.

It was Ann who broke the silence. 'It would have been just too good to happen.'

Nicola understood very well what she meant. To be a part of this delightful family where she fitted in as if she really was 'my cousin Nicola' as Wayne so often called her ... Why did it have to be like this? She had a feeling that Wayne's feeling for her was already something a little more than attraction. Maybe had she not fallen in love with Keith, she might even have come to care, but in her heart she knew that love couldn't be channelled so easily. It came unbidden, and life was never the same again.

True to his promise, John pulled up in the driveway of the beach house one morning. Nicola, on her way down to the beach for a swim, glanced towards him in surprise. 'You look different!' she burst out. Clad in a gaily patterned floral shirt and shorts, a scarlet towelling beach hat pulled over his dark hair, he looked younger, she thought. The set expression she secretly termed his 'lawyer look' had given way to a relaxed happy expression.

'So do you.' His appreciative gaze took in the evenly tanned skin. The long dark hair she washed daily after the dip in salt water was burnished in the rays of hot sunshine.

'It's all this outdoor living, and besides,' she chatted as they moved towards the back door, 'I'm being made such a fuss of here, you wouldn't believe! I'm being absolutely spoiled!'

'Do you good! It is your holiday——'

'Plus investigation job, don't forget. I don't suppose——'

'Nothing's come to hand lately, but don't worry, I'll think of something. We're not giving up the search yet.'

'That's the spirit!'

In the house everyone crowded around John and it was

quite a time before he managed to take Nicola away with him. 'We're off down to the boat harbour,' he told them in parting. 'I want to take Nicola for a run around the bay.'

'You don't know how lucky you are, young man,' Wayne's father told him. 'If it hadn't been that Wayne happens to be on duty at the clubhouse today, you wouldn't have got a look-in. Isn't that right, Nicola?'

'He's being so good taking me around.'

'Good? Is that what you call it?' Mrs Fletcher put in with her broad smile, 'I wouldn't say he was fighting too hard to do his duty!'

'I'm a sort of adopted cousin,' Nicola said, as they left the house in a chorus of laughter and teasing remarks.

'They treat everyone like that who comes to stay,' Nicola said as they took the winding path towards the sand hills, 'they're so kind——'

'Especially Wayne?'

She laughed and said, 'What would you like to do first? There are endless things to do here, swimming, sunbathing, or go out in the boat?'

'Spoken like a real Kiwi, but after the drive, I'll settle for a swim.'

'Me too.' They had reached the expanse of sand, already hot to the touch of their bare feet. 'I usually go in just about here.'

'Right,' John was stripping off his shirt. 'Race you in!'

Nicola dropped her towelling beach wrap on the sand. 'I'm not so sure that I want to be first in!'

'You will be, though!' John had picked up a handful of wet seaweed and mindful of him in swift pursuit, Nicola sped along the beach. She was a good sprinter, but so was he, and at last she swerved suddenly and ran into the tossing spray.

The next moment he was splashing after her, to catch her in his arms, and despite her screams of protest, he strode resolutely through the waves, to dump her in the way of an oncoming breaker. The green wall of water submerged her, but at last she emerged, breathless and laughing, her hair streaming around her.

'Beast!' She braced her feet against the drag of the wave.

'You asked for it!' He dived through a breaker.

As Nicola dashed the water from her eyes, she found herself meeting the gaze of a girl who was standing in the shallows. Surely it was Sharon? The next moment the girl turned away to pick up a rubber mattress and hurry along the beach.

Nicola called to John, 'Wasn't that Sharon?'

He spun around in the water, his voice sharp, 'Where?'

'There! That girl by herself carrying a rubber mattress, going along the beach.'

At that moment, however, a crowd of picnickers obscured the view and when they caught sight of the girl again, she was too far away to be recognised.

John looked after the hurrying figure. 'It couldn't have been Sharon. She never cared for this coast. When she goes for a dip it's out to the Waihi beach.' A nostalgic note coloured his tone. 'We used to swim there a lot—last summer.' The next moment he was smiling again. 'A swim, I said, not riding the breakers!'

'I like it this way, it's fun! Look out——' Nicola broke off as a wall of water, white-crested, thundered towards them and in the split second as it surged past she dropped down, to be carried inshore on the force of the wave.

As always on the sun-washed beach, the hours went by like minutes, Nicola thought, but at last they waded out of the sea. Much later, when they had sunbathed on the sand, they strolled together along the beach. Today there weren't many people about, a few picnic parties and odd groups of girls and men. Once, glancing back, Nicola caught sight of a girl with head bent and eyes downcast, who was walking along the sand. She was almost certain the girl was Sharon and she was about to mention the matter to John, but when she glanced back again the girl, whoever she was, had turned away and was hidden in the sandhills. Oh well, she might have been mistaken.

The water foamed over their feet as they splashed along in the shallows, passing the sea lane reserved for water-skiers and waving to Wayne, on duty in the high tower overlooking the long expanse of beach.

Presently they reached the sheltered inlet where thickly-growing bush crowded down the hillside to meet its own reflection in calm water. Gaily painted craft, motor boats, yachts and catamarans, rocked gently at their moorings.

John had climbed aboard the red and white runabout when Nicola, waiting on the shore, spied a figure lying on a rubber mattress, some distance out at sea. Chances were, she told herself, that the adventurous lad wasn't in any real danger, but it was possible that he could be drifting out to sea and with this stiff off shore breeze blowing ... 'John!' she called, 'there's someone out there on a li-lo and he seems to be a fair way out at sea!'

He gave a swift glance over the tossing waves. 'Just as well to take a look-see. He could be drifting out on the ebb tide without realising it. I'd better make sure he's not in trouble. Wait there, won't be long!' The next moment the motor roared into life and the runabout hurtled out of the sheltered boat harbour.

A hand held to her eyes to shade the glare of brilliant sunlight, Nicola stood watching as the runabout shot over the water towards the mattress bobbing amongst the waves. How fortunate that John had gone to the rescue, she mused, for even as she watched, she caught sight of an arm raised in a distress signal. The next moment the slight figure on the li-lo was beckoning towards the man at the wheel of the speeding boat. No doubt, she mused, the lad on the li-lo had paddled far out to sea before he realised the danger, but he would be safe now with help at hand. Doubtless Wayne would be watching the scene from his viewing platform in the clubhouse, one rescue he would have no need to take part in. From the shore, it appeared as though John was having some difficulty in getting the boy on to the runabout, but at last he was aboard.

There were few people about in the boat harbour, only a few boat-owners working on their craft, as John sped back in a flurry of white spray. As John pulled the boat up into the shallows Nicola hurried to meet him, then stopped abruptly. Too late she recognized Sharon's slim figure and sandy-coloured hair. The glance the other girl sent her was tight with anger.

'Hello,' Nicola faltered, 'are you all right?'

Sharon shook drops of water from her hair. 'You can see for yourself, can't you?'

Nicola decided to ignore the other girl's sullen stare. She sent John a bright smile, at least she hoped it was bright. 'Wayne will be annoyed with you for butting in on his territory. Going after people before he has a chance to know whether they really need rescuing or not!'

Sharon's face was pale and set. 'Of course I needed help. You saw my distress signal, didn't you? That's right, isn't it, John?' She appealed to the man at her side.

But only when you saw John was near. The sneaky thought intruded in Nicola's mind. The next moment she was struck by a pang of pity. Sharon's face was so pale and wan and her eyes held an expression of desperate hopelessness. She realized it was useless for her to extend any friendliness. The other girl's jealousy blinded her to anything else. Sharon was determined to hate her.

'Well, so long as you're all right,' said Nicola, and turned away. 'Me, I'm off for a spot of sunbathing.' The other two scarcely seemed to notice as she slipped away.

The sandhills were hot to her bare feet and once out of sight of the sheltered inlet she spread her towel on the marram grass growing over the dunes and sank down, delighted in the sun's warmth on her skin. Sheltered by the sea breeze, it was very still, the only sound the crying of the gulls soaring in the blue bowl of the sky and the endless surge and drag of the surf. Dreamily she lay gazing at the bush-clad hills above the inlet. They were so good to her up at the house, but just for once it was pleasant to be alone with her thoughts. Pleasant, that was, if she didn't allow her mind to dwell on Keith. Immediately she broke the resolution. Now if only he had been with her at this holiday at the beach....

She drifted away on a dream, to be jerked back to reality by the echo of voices. A girl's voice reached her, low and tense and charged with emotion. Nicola considered getting to her feet and making her escape, but it was already too late. She recognised John's measured tones and knew that the couple must be quite close, probably on the other side of the sandhill.

Sharon had raised her tone. 'I might have known it was no use talking to you. You can think of nothing but *her*!'

John's calm rejoinder: 'How about remembering you've got Nicola to thank for getting you picked up just now? She was the one who spotted you first and saw you were in trouble.'

'Rubbish! I could easily have paddled back, if I'd wanted to.'

So, Nicola mused, it was as she had suspected, all a trick on Sharon's part. Half out of her senses with misery and jealousy, she had made a desperate bid to win back John's affections, only to make a fool of herself. The situation between them now was worse than ever. Nicola felt like telling the stupid girl that John wasn't seriously interested in her, but she knew that in her present mood of resentment, Sharon would never believe her.

'That's what you think! Anyone would get the idea you wanted to drift out to sea. You don't seem to realise,' he stormed, 'you might have drowned!'

Nicola barely caught the low distressed words. 'Would you have cared?'

'Of course I'd have cared!'

'But not enough. You'd have forgotten me by tomorrow, now that you have *her*.'

'Oh, don't be an idiot!' John sounded as though he was fast losing patience. 'Nicola's a nice kid, we get on fine. I'd be a pretty low character if I didn't try to entertain her a bit after she'd come all this way for a visit.'

'Entertaining her? Is that what you call it? Being with her every night of the week at your home, then when she moves out here you have to follow. Do you know what they're saying in town about you and that girl? I heard them talking the other day, a couple in a coffee lounge in the town. "You know," they said, "the girl from England, *John Hazlett's girl*!"'

'Oh, come off it, Shar,' John's voice was that of someone soothing an over-excited person. 'You've got yourself into a state over nothing!'

'Have I? I'll tell you something that might be news to you. You're wasting your time with that one! She likes all the men. You must have noticed. Anyone can see young Wayne Fletcher is badly smitten, and even Keith Lorimer was taken in by her, for a time, until he saw through her. Catch him joining in the rush to escort Nicola Ayres around the place! She's using you, anyone can see it, anyone who isn't blind and deaf——'

'Shut up, will you?' Placid, even-tempered John was shouting.

'Don't, John! I thought,' moaned Sharon, 'that if you had to come and rescue me, you'd feel ... like you used to ...' she choked on the words. Suddenly all the anger and jealousy she was feeling seemed to come to a head and her voice rose out of control. 'It's all because of her! You were different to me before she came here. She's bewitched you!'

John's level tone held a hint of anxiety. 'Calm down, Shar. You're right off beam about Nicola.' Nicola could imagine his worried expression. 'I like her all right, but——'

'Don't lie to me! I know how you *really* feel about her!'

'Listen to me——' Nicola could picture John's bewildered look, 'forget Nicola! How about coming out with me for a run in the boat? We could take a look around the next bay, maybe do a spot of fishing. You used to like fishing.'

'I hated it! I only pretended to like it because you wanted me to.' The angry tone changed. 'I just wanted to be with you.'

'Just come out for a run, then?'

Sharon's voice, half mollified, half sulky. 'Will *she* be coming?'

'Nicola? If I can find her. She could be anywhere along the beach.'

'Well, I'm not then.'

A silence, then John's exasperated voice. 'Don't be like this, Shar. It's not like you.'

'It's not like you either, running around with *her* all the time!'

The voices seemed closer and for a tense moment Nicola wondered if the couple were approaching the spot where she was hidden behind a great drift of sand. The next moment, however, the sounds faded. Nicola waited for a few minutes, then got to her feet and made her way back over the sandhills in the direction of the house.

Poor Sharon, her thoughts ran as she plodded through drifts of sand; someone should tell her that pleading and recriminations were scarcely the best way in which to win back a man's love. But how could one reason when there was only the longing that blinded one to everything else, including common sense. The trouble was, unconsciously she sighed, you couldn't argue love away, you couldn't even talk any sense into yourself! *Look who's talking!*

For Nicola now, the days merged into a haze of endless activity. Sometimes Wayne's two married sisters teased her about it. 'You certainly know how to keep 'em guessing,' Ann told her. 'No jealousy, no hard feelings——'

'And so well planned too,' Merle chimed in. 'Mornings while Wayne is on duty on the beach, you're out boating with John. Afternoons are Wayne's time. He's the one she goes swimming and sunbathing with.'

'And this is the girl who used to help us out minding the kids half the day,' Ann complained with mock-disappointment. 'Now I have to take them down to the beach myself in the mornings and run after beach balls, not to mention changing their wet clothes half a dozen times a day. How did I know that my mother's help would turn into the most popular girl on the beach?'

Nicola joined in the laughter. 'I've got to collect a suntan to take back to England with me somehow!'

As always, at mention of her departure, so soon now,

only a few weeks ahead, the laughter died away. They couldn't care as much as I do about my leaving here, she thought, when I'm leaving Keith for ever.

Late one morning she was alone on the beach when Wayne, his morning duties at the surf club ended, came hurrying towards her. As she went to meet him he took her hand in his. 'I thought the time would never go, I've been counting the hours until I could be with you.'

She smiled up into the bronzed face. 'No exciting rescues?'

'*You* are my excitement,' he whispered. He was gazing down at her with an expression that told her so much more than he realised. No wonder his family were thinking that he had fallen in love at last. How can I let him down easily? she thought. He's been so good to me and if he really feels the way I think he does, he's going to be hurt badly after I've gone.

As she made to move on, he dropped to the warm sand and pulled her down at his side. 'Don't go, stay here with me.' His hand came down on hers and he put her fingers to his lips. 'I know so little about you, you never talk about yourself.'

Lazily she stared up at the translucent blue sky high above. 'What is it you want to know?'

'What you do when you're at home. Where you go. Friends, amusements, the lot?'

She watched a light plane skimming over the water. 'It all sounds so ordinary really, now I come to think about it. Girl is brought up by an aunt——'

'Why an aunt?'

'Girl's parents were killed in a motor smash when she was a child.'

'Tough luck, a crusty old aunt.'

Nicola turned on her stomach, letting the sand sift through her fingers. 'But my aunt's a darling. We get on fine. If it hadn't been for her, I wouldn't be here right now.'

'I withdraw all criticism, I'm all for your aunt!'

'So you should be! She's the one who's anxious to find

out what happened to her brother, last heard of in Waihi, New Zealand, umpteen years ago, So far,' her voice was rueful, 'I don't seem to have been much help. Between us, John and I seem to have just about exhausted all the avenues we can think of in the search-for-Uncle-Walter project.'

'Oh, John——!' His tone was derisive.

'No, honestly,' she said defensively. 'He's been a great help—and don't look at me like that,' she teased, 'just because I was staying at his home. It was the only address I had in the country and I do work at the office of a family friend. Work' ... her voice was dreamy, 'I can scarcely believe I have to go back, leaving all this. The warmth, the clear air, the way the sunlight sparkles on the water. I try to write home and tell them, but I can't seem to really describe the atmosphere, the summery feeling of it all, can't find the words somehow——'

'Don't go back,' his deep tones, husky with emotion, cut across her reverie. 'You don't have to. Stay here with me, marry me.'

'*Marry you?*' Nicola shot up into a sitting position, staring down at him incredulously. The eyes she was gazing into weren't laughing but shadowed with feeling.

'I mean it. We could have a great life together, you and me. The family's no problem, you get on fine with them and they all think the sun shines out of you. You love this beach life——'

But I don't love you, not in the one important way, not enough. The thought rushed into her mind.

Aloud she began inadequately, 'I'm sorry ...'

'It's my fault,' he said quickly, 'I've rushed my fences. It's only because I have to move fast or it will be too late. Sometimes it hits me that time's running out and if I don't do something about it, one day soon you'll have left me.' His voice thickened and she barely caught the low words, 'and I'll never see you again.' Once again he carried her hand to his lips. 'Why won't you say yes?'

In the silence he flung himself angrily aside. 'It's that guy over in England that's the trouble, isn't it?'

Nicola let him think it was the truth; it was easier that way.

Moodily Wayne studied her downcast face. 'I wouldn't care so much if you were happy about the fellow, but there's something wrong, isn't there, something you're not letting on about?'

'You're far too perceptive for a beach boy!' Her smile belied the shadow in her eyes.

'Listen,' he caught her hands in his strong clasp, 'if there's anything I can do to help, or if I've got any hope of getting what I want, you'll let me know—promise?'

'I promise.'

'But there's something you can do for me,' all at once his tone was eager, entreating, 'just stay on here with us until you have to go away,' he swallowed, 'if you must go.'

'That's easy.' Mrs Fletcher and her daughters had put the same question to her only this morning and Nicola was only too glad to accept the invitation to extend her stay. That way she would be in no danger of running into Keith, as would be the case in Waihi. And wasn't that what she wanted, to be free of him—if she could. Aloud she said, 'I'll tell John tomorrow that I'm staying on here, I know he'll understand.'

'That gives me a bit more time to be with you. I might be lucky yet.' She made no answer and for once Wayne did not pursue the subject. 'Tell you what I'll do,' she raised her eyes to meet his ardent gaze, 'I'll take you over to my island.'

'Bribery will get you nowhere—and how do you mean, "your island"?'

'It's just the way I happen to feel about it. Very few boats have ever called in there. For one thing, you can only make your way through the passage in dead calm weather, the swell's too high to get inside otherwise.'

Nicola looked up to a sky of cloudless blue, then her gaze swept the calmest of seas. 'You mean, this sort of day?'

He nodded. 'Preferably with my sort of girl to take along.'

She said quickly, 'Is it one of those three tiny islands off the foreshore?'

'The smallest one. It looks solid from here, but when you get there you find it's open to the sky, a miniature atoll. I'll show you.'

His boat was near and soon the runabout was hurtling over green depths as the spray rose around them, and they plunged on in the direction of the tiny islands ahead. Before long, Wayne cut the engine and they were gliding into a cave with fern-encrusted rock walls.

Nicola stepped out of the boat to find herself standing on a miniature sandy beach. Looking around her in wonder, she saw that the island was indeed open to the sky for pale sunlight filtered through ferns and bushes crowding high above.

'I've never seen anything like it,' she breathed, and stooped to pick up a shell from the tiny strip of sand beneath her feet.

He came to stand at her side. 'You haven't seen it all yet.' He took her hand in his strong clasp and they went through a smaller cave. Then Wayne was pushing aside thickly growing green bushes and tree ferns and Nicola blinked in the sunshine pouring down on the other side of the tiny island. Presently they turned and made their way back through the cave, their voices echoing in the stillness, then they were in a larger opening, enclosed by damp, fern-encrusted rock walls.'

'It's a magic place!' Nicola was splashing her feet in the coolness of the shallow water lapping against the sand. Shafts of sunlight slanting through the greenery overhead threw shadows on Wayne's face, making him appear older, more serious, than the lighthearted companion she knew so well. Suddenly he was close behind her, his arms thrown around her shoulders, his husky voice in her ear. 'Why do you think I brought you here? I want to *make* you care! Stay with me, Nicola. Don't go, don't ever go away. We're always with such a mob of people at home. Down on the beach and at dances at the clubhouse, I never seem to get you to myself ... to kiss you ... the way I want to.'

Before she could make a reply his lips, hard and demanding, were pressed close to hers. His lingering kiss didn't really register with her, just a kiss from which at last she pulled herself free. He leaned back against the rock wall. Was it the gloom of the cave that lent his face that sulky, immature look? 'I don't spark off any excitement with you, do I? I could be any man, except him, that guy in England that you're so absorbed in. Admit it!'

'I——'

'Don't bother trying to let me down lightly, it's not your fault. You can't help being—just you.' The anguish in his voice touched her, but what could she say?

'But I'm not giving up.' All at once there was a note of optimism in his tones, 'not until I say goodbye to you at Auckland airport.'

'I wish it didn't have to be this way,' she whispered.

'Don't be sorry,' his voice had lost its bitter tinge, 'I'm not taking no for an answer—you do like me?'

She said very low, 'You know I do.'

'Right.'

They climbed back into the runabout and slowly and carefully Wayne guided the craft through the narrow opening, the waves breaking around them.

As they emerged into full sunlight, a great white pleasure craft swept towards them. A crowd of people lined the deck, but Nicola was aware of only the man and woman leaning against the railing. The next moment her heart gave a leap, then settled again as she found herself meeting Keith's startled gaze. What was he thinking? She lifted a hand in answer to the waving passengers and was still staring after the powerful motorboat as it sped away.

She became aware of Wayne's curious glance. 'Someone you know?'

She nodded. 'Just Keith Lorimer—and Annabel.'

Thank heaven, she thought, Wayne hadn't caught the

odd note in her voice. To think, she mused on a sigh, that she had actually hoped she might be getting over that particular madness—but one glimpse of Keith's face and the ache of longing was back, stronger than ever.

CHAPTER NINE

As the night of Jane's sixteenth birthday party drew near, it seemed to Nicola that the whole family became affected by the prevailing excitement. Jane's father grumbled good-naturedly at the mounting cost of toll calls, not to mention being unable to make use of the telephone when he wished, but Jane took no notice.

'You did send Keith Lorimer an invitation?' Jane asked her mother one morning at breakfast. 'Funny that he hasn't replied.'

Her mother, spooning cereal into the open mouth of a two-year-old grandson, looked up. 'No, I thought you'd done that, you talk so much about him that I never dreamed——'

'Mum!' Jane wailed in horror. 'It's too late now. He mightn't come.'

'Ring him up, then,' came her mother's placid tones, 'if you're so worried about him.'

'I can't! He'll think I'm chasing after him!'

Her voice was drowned by the derisive laughter of her sisters. Wayne asked teasingly, 'What do you call it?'

Jane lifted her small chin. 'It's just that I'm short of older men. I don't want a lot of kids.'

'I'm hitting twenty-nine,' Wayne pointed out, 'and Keith Lorimer looks to be about the same vintage. A lot of the club crowd are heading that way. Why don't you ask them along?'

'I don't want all of your stupid surf club, they'll be here anyway, most of them. I only want——'

'Don't forget you'll have to ask Annabel along too,' her

brother reminded her with brutal frankness. 'He never goes anywhere much without her these days, so I'm told.'

'I know.' Jane's face fell, then lightened with a sudden hope. 'But she might not be in Waihi. Isn't the Gown of the Year contest on in Wellington next weekend? I was reading about it in the papers. She could be away.' She flung an imploring glance towards her mother. 'Ask him right away, Mum. It's getting late for invitations and if he has another engagement that night, I'll die, I'll just *die*!'

Mrs Fletcher sighed resignedly. 'I suppose I'll have to.'

'Now, Mum, please! I'll feed Tony. You might catch Keith before he goes to work at the mill.'

'May as well get it over with,' her mother grumbled, and got up to go to the telephone.

Nicola found that she was holding her breath. She hoped that Keith would have a prior engagement for the night of the party, or pretend he had. No, she didn't. The longing never far away spread right through every part of her. Just to see him again, to hear his voice ... Not that he would be the slightest bit interested in her, not after the knockbacks she had given him, *had* to give him. I didn't want to treat you that way Keith, she thought, but I had to, and you'll never know. She wrenched her mind back to sanity. What would he care about her anyway? Not much, nor anything, probably.

Mrs Fletcher's friendly tones cut through her musing. 'A birthday party ... our youngest daughter Jane, I think you met her on the beach the other day. We wondered if you'd care to come along next Saturday night? Just a few friends ... You will? She'll be so pleased!' Behind her mother's back Jane was making triumphant gestures. 'You'll bring Annabel along with you?' A pause. 'Oh, that's a pity, perhaps another time. We'll see you here, then. Goodbye.' She turned away from the telephone. 'He said he'll be delighted to come, and he's sorry but Annabel will be away at the Gown of the Year contest.'

'Super!' Jane whirled around the room. I can have him all to myself!'

Her mother was unimpressed. 'He's far too old for anyone of your age to be interested in——'

'Oh, *Mum*!' Jane sent her mother a pitying glance, 'you don't understand!'

Mrs Fletcher, however, was accustomed to the familiar words and took no notice.

'I only want to dance with him,' Jane told her indignantly. 'What's wrong with that?'

'Nothing, nothing,' agreed her mother with long-suffering patience.

Nicola was thinking in panic, If I dance with him I'll be lost. I won't be able to hide the way I feel about him and he'll see, he'll know——

'Look at Nicola,' Jane's laughing tones pierced her wild jumble of thoughts, 'she stayed right there in the house with the man and forgot all about him the next day!'

If they only knew, Nicola thought, and conscious of all eyes turned in her direction, managed to give a fair imitation of a light and careless laugh.

The next morning the rain came, pelting down on the iron roof with the force and suddenness of an electrical storm. Lightning zigzagged over the windows and thunder rolled in from the moist dark clouds hanging over the sea. Something of the wild grandeur of the scene outside matched her own restless mood. There would be no water-skiing with Wayne today, that was for sure. Pulling a hooded waterproof jacket over her shoulders, she wandered down to the clubhouse where Wayne was on duty, watching beside him in the high terrace, the waves crashing up on the sand, driven by high winds and long spears of rain.

After a time she left him to return to the house where she found Jane deep in the intricacies of home dressmaking. Pattern pieces were spread over the floor as she studied the instructions, shouting all the time at the children not to walk on the flimsy tissue.

At last Ann, a competent sewer, came to her rescue and Jane seated herself at the sewing machine as she ran up the seams that Ann had pinned in place.

'I had to give her a hand,' Ann grinned towards Nicola, 'or we'd never have a chance to use the sewing machine.

Merle and I are making dresses to. We thought we'd better run up something new for Jane's precious party. I suppose,' a note of envy tinged her tone, 'you've brought swags of gorgeous gear with you from London?'

'Not really. Just a long floral skirt and muslin blouse and a black dress for evenings like this one.'

'A little black dress? That could be dangerous!' Merle laughed. 'Wayne had better look out for himself!'

'It isn't all that glamorous. Just a dress that I made in a last-minute rush at home, before I had to leave for the airport.'

'You don't look all that excited about the party,' Ann took in the droop of Nicola's lips. 'Bet you'd be feeling a bit different about it all if he could be here with you Saturday night?'

'He?' Nicola's pulses gave a traitorous leap.

'The man you've left behind you, the one you're going back to when you leave us for good.' She sent Nicola a shrewd look. 'Or was Wayne having us on?'

Nicola put on her gayest smile. 'You should know, he's your brother!'

'I asked your friend John to come along to the party,' Jane told her one day that week. 'I happened to run into him along the beach and he promised he'd come.'

During the following few days the sewing machine whirred endlessly as Jane's blue dress, Ann's golden caftan and Merle's rose-patterned skirt gradually took shape. Jane, on trying on her finished effort, threw the garment angrily to the floor and vowed she wouldn't be seen dead in it. 'If only that Annabel would start a boutique in her own home town,' she said crossly. 'Everyone says she's planning one, but what's the use of that to me right now!' She hurried away to try to persuade her mother to take her into town and buy her a ready-made garment.

The frantic sewing activities of the last few days now gave way to long baking and sandwich-making sessions. Snowy white Pavlovas were taken from the oven in readiness for the following day when they would be piled high with mounds of fresh cream and decorated with Kiwi

fruit, whose flavour, Nicola had found, was as delicate as
the silvery green texture of the furry-skinned fruit.

The next evening, Nicola stood with Jane and the rest
of the family at the open doorway, welcoming guests
who were crowding into the house. No one, looking at
the smiling dark-haired girl, could have guessed that the
evening ahead meant anything more to her than a pleasant
social occasion, rather than a bittersweet ordeal that somehow must be got through without betraying her heartache.

In the spacious area below the main part of the house,
rugs had been tossed aside and the floor polished for
dancing. Trestle tables were arranged at one end of the
room and through doors open to the sea breeze, stereo
music drifted out to drown the dull boom of the surf
on the beach below. The heat of the day had given way
to the cool of evening and a few stars pricked the velvety
blue-blackness of the night sky.

Soon the wide driveway was filled with parked vehicles
and cries of 'Happy birthday, Jane' and 'Where's the
birthday girl?' echoed around the room. A low coffee table
was piled high with paper wrappings as Jane, with smiles
of thanks and appreciation, opened up the varied gift
parcels. Amongst the throng around her she stood out, a
radiant figure, sun-tanned shoulders rising from tiers of
diaphanous material of her creamy-coloured dress, her only
jewellery a pearl hanging from a gold chain, that had
been Nicola's birthday gift.

'This dress cost the earth,' she had confided to Nicola
the day before. 'It's got an "Annabel Gown" label, and
you know what that means! Mum didn't want to pay so
much, but I talked her into letting me have it as a birthday present! I never dreamed we'd find anything like it,
so close to home!'

Presently couples began moving towards the dance
floor and from that moment Nicola found herself besieged
with partners. In her short stay in the district she had
already got to know the Surf Club members and would
have danced with each in turn had not Wayne stayed

determinedly at her side, leading her away the moment the dance music started once again, before any of his mates could claim her.

After a time Jane came hurrying towards them. 'I thought,' she told Wayne in a fierce whisper, 'you were supposed to be in the bar tonight?'

'Get someone else to do it,' he replied carelessly, 'I'm not leaving Nicola.'

'If that's the way you feel about it.' Jane shrugged her shoulders and moved away in search of a more amenable bartender.

Nicola didn't mind in the least dancing exclusively with Wayne. She went through the familiar movements to the beat of the pop tunes as if in a dream, but she couldn't help her glance straying endlessly towards the entrance. As time went by, however, she told herself she was glad that Keith had evidently decided not to come here tonight. The next moment a splinter of delight shot through her as she caught sight of him. As always, he seemed to stand out amongst the group of men around him. There was something about him, she mused, a charisma, or could it be just that he looked so tall and erect, so sure of himself that he commanded respect? He was standing motionless just inside the doorway, his glance raking the crowded dance floor. Then the music seemed to soar and swell as for a heart-stopping moment his gaze locked with hers. Keith, alone and searching for her in the crowded room! With an effort of will, she wrenched her glance aside.

At that moment Jane ran forward to greet the new arrival, and soon the two were dancing together. That would make Jane's night, Nicola reflected. Close on the thought came another: Stupid me, acting just like a silly teenager, hoping he'll dance with me! Deliberately she forced herself to dwell on the house plans being drawn up for the home Keith would soon be sharing with Annabel. It worked, bringing her back to reality with a jerk. She vowed to herself she wouldn't dance with him tonight, no, not if he begged her.

He didn't beg, he didn't even ask, but took her completely by surprise, for a little later as music once more flooded through the room, a deep voice beside her said, 'Mine, I think!' Disregarding Wayne's proprietorial gesture and just as if he had every right to be with her, Keith led her away,· his hand clasping hers in a firm grip.

The music happened to be an old-fashioned waltz and Nicola felt bitterly ashamed of the wild sweetness flooding her as he held her close, blissfully close. Heaven to be near him once again! How many times in dreams had this happened—but this wasn't a dream, she told herself over the tumult of her senses. Before she realised his intention he had circled her towards the entrance, then he drew her out into the cool night air. A salty breeze cooled her hot cheeks and stirred the hair on her forehead as his hand closed once more over hers and he led her down the track towards the beach. It *would* be a night like this, she thought wildly as he led her down over drifts of sand. A full moon threw a pathway over the sea and above them the Milky Way was a silver dusting of stars.

'Now,' he tucked her arm in his and they strolled along the sands, deserted now, except for themselves, 'I've got you to myself at last!'

She fought against the wild excitement that threatened to make her forget the really important things, like Annabel. 'Why don't you leave me alone?' she whispered.

His voice was a caress. 'Do you really want me to? Come on, Nicola,' he said softly, 'be honest with me for once. One minute I could swear you wanted me around, then you change into another girl that I can't fathom.'

'It's your own fault,' she said thickly, almost indistinctly. 'Why are you following me around?'

'I have to, it's the only chance I've had in weeks to see you and get you to myself.'

'Another girl to hang around you mean?' The words seemed to come without her volition.

'Another girl?' His puzzled tone changed to one of relief. 'If you're talking about your friend Jane, don't tell me you don't recognise a schoolgirl crush when you see one?'

'I don't mean Jane,' she said very low. Did she have to spell it out to him? Strange that he actually seemed at a loss to understand what must be perfectly obvious to him. Didn't understand or didn't want to admit the truth?

'I got the quaint idea,' he was saying, 'that the invitation to come along tonight was your idea ... I couldn't think of any other reason why Fletchers should ask me along. I don't even know them.'

'Can't you?' Could that be her own voice, so sarcastic and horrible? It just went to show the effect that frustration and a feeling of betrayal could have on you. 'You're quite a presentable male, you know!'

Too late she realised it had been the wrong thing to say, for he took the words as an invitation and turned sharply towards her, an exultant sound in his deep tones. 'You never told me you felt that way about me before.'

Hurriedly she quickened her steps. 'I'm not telling you now. I'm just passing on what Jane thinks about you.'

'Jane? Oh yes, the kid sister.'

'That's the one. She wheedled her mother into asking you along tonight. It seems,' she hated herself for the barbed note in her voice, 'that she'd heard about you and one look at you on the beach the other day and she'd gone overboard for you ... like all the others.'

His voice was dangerously quiet. 'What do you mean?'

She realised she had gone too far and tried to retrieve the hastily spoken words. 'Oh, you know, wherever I go I keep hearing how all the girls are longing to meet you. You should have heard Jane's sisters talking——'

'Jane's sisters? I don't know them.'

'Oh, that makes no difference! Everyone's heard of Keith Lorimer up at Sky Lodge. You've got yourself quite a reputation around this part of the country.'

'What's got into you, Nicola?' All at once his voice was husky with emotion. 'There's only one girl I happen to be interested in, and she——'

'I know, I know! Don't tell me!' Nicola couldn't bear to have to listen to him proudly recounting Annabel's achievements, her beauty, all over again. Her face was flushed, her voice rising out of control. 'I'd better get back to the house,' she turned and began to hurry away, 'Wayne will be sending out a search party for me.'

'Wayne!' Keith caught up with her in a couple of long strides and swung her around to face him. 'So that's the way it is! I've heard rumours about you and Wayne, but I refused to believe them.' He released her so abruptly that she all but fell. 'Still planning on going back to England?'

'Yes, I am.'

'Well then, you're not too much involved with him.' His tone dropped to the dangerously caressing note against which she had no defence. 'Come here, Nicola!'

Trembling, she glanced back over her shoulder. He was standing motionless on the sands. Was it the moonglow that lent his face dark planes of shadow? 'I could make you love me,' he said softly, 'and you know it!'

'I don't love anyone——'

'Liar,' he breathed softly, 'I've seen the way you look at me, when you're not running away! Why do you run away? You must know that we were made for each other!'

It was surging over her once again, the weakness that made her long to stay in his arms for ever. Even as she felt herself falling in surrender to the dangerous sweetness of the moment, a couple came strolling towards them, two shadows on the sand. For Nicola, the moonlit world swung back into focus and she had the feeling of coming back from somewhere a long way away. It was a journey that could have ended only in disillusionment and despair, so how could she wish that they two had remained alone on the moonlit beach? Surely, she thought wildly, a girl in love should be allowed one last kiss, even Annabel couldn't begrudge her that. But in her heart she was aware that once in Keith's arms, his lips on hers, she would come perilously close to abandoning her convictions and nothing in all the world would matter, not even Annabel.

The couple passed them by, but still Keith made no move to catch up with her. 'Nicola, come back! There's something I've got to say to you——'

But she was back in control of herself. If she didn't stay close to him she'd be safe. If she couldn't hear his spoken words she wouldn't be tempted to remain with him in the intimacy of the soft darkness.

'Come back!' he called. But she had gained the entrance to the flight of steps and was hurrying towards the lighted room above.

At the open doors at the top of the landing, Wayne was waiting for her. 'I've been looking for you all over,' He drew her towards the dance floor and they moved to the beat of the latest pop tune. 'You're trembling, what's wrong?' There was a note of genuine concern in his tones. 'Did someone scare you out there in the dark?—because if they did, just give me the word and I'll go and knock some sense into him!'

'No, no, nothing like that. Maybe I got a chill. The room was so hot, I dashed outside for a breath of fresh air, that was all.'

At that moment Keith came strolling into the room. He looked as detached as ever, Nicola thought, and as always he walked with an air, as if he owned the whole world and could have the love of any girl he fancied, and Annabel as well. She lifted her rounded chin. But not this girl!

At that moment Wayne was called away. She scarcely noticed his going, for Keith was striding purposefully in her direction. Another part of her mind registered Jane's glance, darting from Keith to herself. The next moment he was standing at her side and some devil prompted her to say, 'Why don't you give Jane a dance? You've no idea how grateful she'd be!'

'I'd rather dance with you,' he said, and swept her into the scintillating pattern of dancers moving on the polished floor. At that moment the tune changed once again to the tempo of an old-time waltz, no doubt for the benefit of the older guests. Nicola was glad that she had taken lessons in ballroom dancing and even more glad that Keith was her partner. She hadn't wanted to dance with him—well, she had tried not to want to ... It was no use. She ceased to struggle with her conscience and instead gave herself up to the enchantment of the moment, his arms holding her, his breath stirring the hair at her temple. Deep inside her, something told her that the memory would stay with her all her life, even were she half a world away! All at once she became aware that the music had died into silence and, dazedly, she brought herself back to reality. Soon Keith was leaving her, crossing the floor to merge into a group of men standing at the far end of the room.

As the evening wore on, Nicola danced with Wayne, then with John, and reversed the order. Between dances she supposed she chatted and smiled and made intelligent noises, for no one showed any surprise at anything she said. Once when she and Wayne were standing together there was a pause in the buzz of chatter around them and a girl's clear, carrying voice reached her. 'It isn't *fair*! What is it the English girl's got that we haven't?' She's got *two* men dancing attendance on her tonight. They says it's the same wherever she goes. And the funny thing about it is that she doesn't seem to try, or even care all that much.'

Another voice, feminine, thoughtful. 'Maybe that's her secret! You can't help liking her, though, she's nice.'

'You're telling me! Wayne doesn't even seem to know I'm in the same room since she came to stay with his folks.'

Interested in spite of herself, Nicola strained her ears to catch the conversation. 'Don't worry,' came the consoling voice of the second speaker, 'they say she's going back to England very soon.'

'Thank heaven for that!'

'Probably got somone waiting for her back home.'

'That's what I'm hoping.'

If Nicola hadn't had other matters on her mind, she would have been amused. At that moment she caught

Wayne's selfconscious grin and realised that he too had overheard the conversation.

During the next hour, Keith didn't dance. Nicola knew because she couldn't keep her gaze from straying towards the best-looking man in the room. Apparently he preferred to spend the time in conversation with a group of other non-dancers, gathered together in the shadows. Had she pierced that cool composure of his at last, made him realise that there was one girl in the room who wasn't falling over herself to dance with him—well, not so he'd notice? Or could it be that he was missing Annabel? Nicola felt a little sick at the thought.

At that moment a girl plucked at Wayne's sleeve. Nicola wondered if the bright-faced young woman was the one whose conversation she had inadvertently overheard. Probably, judging by the expression of sheer happiness that lighted her face as Wayne led her towards the dance floor.

'My turn, I think,' she spun around to see John's smiling face. 'You're so popular tonight it's hard to get near you.'

'Only because of Wayne.'

They joined the moving crowd around them, and he said, 'I've missed our boating the last day or two.'

'Blame the weather.'

'I know, I know, but I've still missed you.'

She laughed and concentrated on the pulsing beat. If only she weren't so *aware* of Keith, she told herself as the evening wore on. He didn't again approach her, who could blame him after the things she had said to him down on the beach? At the supper table, he was seated opposite her and all the time she was conscious of him. In spite of the tempting array of food, she had no appetite and neither, apparently, had he. A little later Jane's father rose from the head of the table, to thank guests for their attendance at his daughter's birthday party, and for the many gifts now piled on Jane's bureau in the bedroom upstairs. Toasts were drunk, the birthday cake was cut amidst a rousing chorus of 'Happy birthday to you!', then dancing began once again.

Now Nicola couldn't see Keith, although her gaze searched the big room.

Jane, coming to her side at that moment, tuned in on her thoughts. 'He's gone,' she said sadly, 'Keith's gone. He said he was sorry but he couldn't stay any longer. I suppose,' she said fiercely, 'it's that Annabel he wants to get back to. He said she was due back in Waihi some time tonight, she was driving through in her car. I bet it was just an excuse. I bet he didn't want to stay any longer, just because *she* wasn't here with him!'

Nicola bit her lip. It was the truth, of course, even Jane could see it. Only a fool like her would endeavour to read another, more personal reason into Keith's having left the party so early.

Daylight was breaking when at last Nicola got to bed. She had helped the family to clear away supper dishes and put the room to rights. Anything to stop herself from thinking, remembering. She had been so ruthless towards Keith, but of course he deserved it. So why was she wasting time in regrets? Sleep was a long time coming and she awoke late, to cloudy skies. A cool, salt-laden breeze wafted in at the cottage windows. Today she had no heart for boating with John, even if he weren't sleeping in late himself. It didn't help her mood any to catch her reflection in the mirror—shadowed eyes and a face pale beneath the tan.

CHAPTER TEN

NICOLA had been down on the beach with John all morning and it wasn't until the tide had turned that she left him to make her way up the sandy track.

Inside the bach, the air was close and stuffy. Nicola moved into the living room to open the windows, then stood motionless, staring at the sandy-haired girl who had risen from a seat on the couch to face her.

'Sharon! What on earth are you doing here?'

'Can't you guess?'

Nicola realised the other girl had a distraught expression. Her face was very pale and her eyes had a strange glitter. She looked, the thought flew through Nicola's mind, as if she hadn't slept all night. Aloud she asked, 'How long have you been waiting?'

'Hours—I don't know. What does it matter? I had to see you. The others in the house don't know I'm here, but the door was unlocked so I came in and waited. I knew you'd be back some time and I——' suddenly her voice broke, 'just had to see you.' Nicola had to strain her ears to catch the low tones, charged with emotion. 'It's not *fair*! John would come back to me if it weren't for you, I know he would!' All at once the troubled tones quickened to anger. 'I wouldn't mind if you cared, but everyone knows you've got a special man of your own back in England. It makes me so *mad*!'

Nicola was becoming very weary of taking the blame for the other girl's frustrations and heartache. 'Oh, Sharon,' all at once she lost patience with her, 'you're so *stupid*! Can't you see——'

'I can see what's in front of my eyes,' came the bitter tones. 'John trailing after you, taking you boating, coming out here to see you every day even though he has to share you with Wayne. Don't think I don't know what's been going on between you two——'

'I wish you did know,' Nicola said exasperatedly, 'instead of making yourself miserable imagining things.'

'Let him go,' Sharon choked over the low words, 'he means nothing to you! You've only got to walk into a room and all the men go for you.'

'You're being ridiculous!'

'Am I? Look at John, *my* John. It makes me sick to see him taking his holidays, spending every spare moment he has running after you.' Her voice thickened with unshed tears. 'Do you know what I heard someone say the other night? "Why don't we invite John's girl to the party?" I thought they meant me, then the penny dropped. Can you imagine how that makes me feel?'

'Sharon, it's not my fault,' protested Nicola.

'Oh, don't give me that! You can't tell me that sort of thing just happens, and you have nothing to do with it. My young brother was the first, that night when you arrived here. He couldn't talk of anything else for days, and I don't suppose you even remember him?'

'Of course I remember Bruce. He took me up to Martha Hill——'

'And he's been raving on about you ever since. If it hadn't been that he's been working miles away he'd be joining the I-love-Nicola club right here. Anyone can see that Wayne Fletcher is badly smitten. Even Keith Lorimer fell for your charms, for a while, until he found you out.'

'Keith?' Nicola caught her breath.

'But I don't care about the others, I only care about John. Please,' Sharon entreated once again, 'let him go. You don't need him around. To you,' she said bitterly, 'he's just another man to hover around you, adoring you, making life easy for you, entertaining you. You have so many men who feel that way about you but he's all I've got.' She added on a sob, 'The only man I ever want.'

Nicola didn't know what to say. 'Truly, it's not my fault.'

'How can you say that?' Anger blazed in the other girl's taut tones. 'After you deliberately destroyed the letters I wrote him?'

'Letters! That's not true!'

'Isn't it? John's mother told me you brought them in from the mail box——'

'So I did, but——'

'You admit it, now that you're in a corner!'

'How can you say such things?'

'It's pretty obvious, isn't it? Oh, I know John's mother hates me. She has it in for any girl who threatens to take her precious son away from her. I know she's pretty devious, but she wouldn't go as far as that!'

Nicola was slow to anger, but now she was furious. 'And

I would? You must be out of your mind to think such things.'

'John never got those letters. You can't get away from that.'

'Oh, what's the use, you'd never believe me, but I wouldn't put too much faith in what John's mother tells you if I were you.' Nicola turned away.

'I wish,' shrilled Sharon, 'that you'd go back to England! I wish you were leaving here tomorrow!'

'Don't worry, I'll go back, just as soon as I find what I'm looking for.'

Sharon's face was convulsed and Nicola realised that the other girl was beside herself with jealousy and rage. 'If you really want to know the truth about your uncle, why don't you ask Keith Lorimer? Get him to show you the old family album that he keeps up at Sky Lodge. My father lived here for thirty years and he remembered it well, he was here at the time it happened——' She stopped short, breathing hard.

Nicola's heart seemed to stop beating, then start again. 'What does he remember?' Her voice was very quiet.

'Nothing, nothing.' All at once Sharon was evasive. Clearly she regretted her outburst of a moment ago. 'Don't take any notice of me. My big mouth.'

'Tell me,' demanded Nicola, 'or I'll go and see your father and ask him about it.'

'You'd have a job to do that—my father died years and years ago. Besides, he didn't *know* anything, I swear it. It was just a suspicion he had at the time, but he always said it happened a long time ago and was best forgotten about. There wasn't a scrap of truth in the story. I keep telling you, you'd be crazy to take any notice of anything I said.

'I was shooting my mouth off,' Sharon was speaking quickly, nervously, 'trying to get you to go away from here, if you must know. Don't take any notice,' her voice broke on a sob, 'I'd say a lot more than that if it would bring John back to me.'

'Getting rid of me wouldn't mean that——'

'But it would help.'

'How do you know?' Nicola was scarcely aware of what she was saying. Her mind was ticking over, trying to remember every word Sharon had said to her. Words flung in anger, yet she felt they had an unmistakable ring of truth. 'You said to ask Keith about Uncle Walter,' she was speaking her thoughts aloud, 'but I have asked him and he couldn't help me one little bit.'

'Well then, that proves it, doesn't it? Maybe you'll believe me now when I tell you I was just trying it on.' Sharon moved to the door, then stood motionless, her hand on the knob. 'It didn't do any good, did it, my coming here, throwing myself on your mercy? I might have known I'd be wasting my time.' She blinked away the tears that threatened to spill from her eyes. 'If you tell him about my coming here, I'll never forgive you!'

'Don't worry——' but Sharon had gone. Nicola heard the angry slam of the back door and moving to the window, she watched as Sharon, barefooted, hurried down the sandy track to the beach. Long after the hurrying figure had gone from sight, Nicola remained motionless, her eyes thoughtful, Sharon's words hammering in her mind.

Ask Keith Lorimer, if you really want to know what happened to your uncle. Nicola didn't know what to think. There was no doubt that Sharon, half out of her mind at the time with jealousy, was capable of any old lie if it would have the effect of sending Nicola out of the other girl's life and back to England. And yet there had been something about the way Sharon had flung the words at her, as if she *knew*.

All at once she remembered something Keith had told her when they had been together at Jane's birthday party. It had been one of those times when she was with him when her ears took in the words, but the heady excitement of his nearness overshadowed everything else in her mind. They had been dancing and he had made some mention of the brilliance of the moonlight outside. 'If the fine weather keeps up I'll be over here again at the beginning of the month. I'm due to cut some pines up in

Golden Valley that week.' His voice, deep and vibrant with subtle undertones, had made her aware of what he was saying. 'Why don't you come with me and have a look around? I could pick you up on my way.' His voice had quickened. 'Come to think of it, it wouldn't be the first time I'd picked you up on a logging truck.' The lingering tenderness in his tone had all but cracked her defences. Somehow, though, she had got the better of the voice in her mind that clamoured, 'Oh I'd love that!' She even managed one of her light, careless smiles. 'Sorry, I'd love to.' That at least was the truth, 'but——'

'It's okay,' his voice was brusque, 'just a thought. Another time maybe.' In her heart she had known there wouldn't be another time, not ever. If only it didn't hurt so to decline his invitation to join him!

Now his words returned to mind and refused to be banished. A visit to Golden Valley, to discover the truth of what Sharon had told her, wouldn't be merely to see him. *Who was she fooling?* Well, anyway, there was something she had to find out and only he could tell her. Were she to try to see him at Sky Lodge, she would be more than likely to run into Annabel, and that was a risk she couldn't afford to take. After all, she told herself, she owed it to herself to find out the truth of the matter and there was so little time left. Deep down where it counted, however, she knew that the longing to see Keith just once more took precedence over every other thought in her mind. Why pretend otherwise? Probably he wouldn't want to see her, not after their stormy parting. It made no difference, she couldn't help herself. The thought of being with him was a bittersweet delight. The others in the house would imagine she had gone down to the beach, all except Wayne, and he would be on duty at the clubhouse almost immediately. So she was free to follow her own inclination, which led always in one direction, and that was wherever Keith happened to be. She *had* to see him and would be glad of any excuse.

Swiftly she showered and changed into a blue sun-dress, the narrow shoulder ties contrasting with the deep tan of her arms and shoulders. Even though heavy gun-metal clouds were massing overhead, heat-clouds John called them, the day was warm and she suspected would become warmer still in the still green depths of the pine filled valley.

She slipped her feet into tan leather sandals and let herself out of the back door. Evidently Wayne had had to hurry back to the clubhouse, she caught a glimpse of him in the distance, and there was no one about. Even the children seemed to be indoors and it was easy to slip away unseen. She had seen the valley from a motorboat. Wayne had pointed it out to her one day when they had been out on the water. 'I'll take you up to Golden Valley one day,' he had promised, 'we'll have ourselves a picnic. Don't let on to the others though, or you know what will happen. It'll turn into a free-for-all and I won't get you to myself for two minutes all day.' Now she was going there alone on a mission that might mean the end of her search, at a time when she had practically given up hope of success. She shied away from the thought of what the explanation might involve, telling herself that Sharon might not have been speaking the truth.

Far ahead she could see the valley, sombre away from the sun, the slopes clothed in symmetrical rows of pines. She was hurrying along the roadway, too intent on her thoughts to be aware of the logging truck that had slowed to a stop at her side.

'Want a lift, lady?'

'Keith!' The caressing note in his deep tones, the sheer bliss of seeing him once again, sent reservations and suspicions fleeing from her mind and there was only Keith, looking at her with the special deep glowing look in his eyes. 'Oh, I do!' Uplifted on a cloud of joy, she climbed up on to the high seat beside him.

'Where are you bound for anyway?' His tone was matter-of-fact, his words just what a driver would say to anyone to whom he was offering a ride, so why was her heart lifting, the windswept cloudy day suddenly quite wonderful?

'You'd never believe this——'

'Try me.' He started the motor and they swept along the road.

'I was coming to see you, actually.'

She was aware of his quick, sideways glance. 'Changed your mind, you mean, about coming with me today?'

She hesitated. 'In a way.' Don't put it to him too soon about what Sharon told me about him. Don't spoil everything, not just yet, not this minute!

Soon they were turning off the main highway and swinging into a side road leading up into pine-covered hills. As Keith guided the logging truck along a dirt road with the dust rising behind them, Nicola commented idly, 'This seems to be a fire break?'

He nodded. 'It's got to be wide so that a fire doesn't jump the distance.'

They were dropping down into a valley when she heard the whine of a chain saw and caught sight of a bulldozer moving amongst the pines. Nicola recognised the driver, a burly figure with massive sun-browned shoulders rising from a black work shirt. He was the bushman who she had seen previously working amongst the trees with Keith. She waved a hand towards him. 'Now I'm getting the idea of it all. The bulldozer driver hauls the logs down to those skids built on the bank and they're piled up there ready to load on to the logging truck, that's your department.'

'You're coming along like wildfire,' he grinned down at her. 'The way you're shaping you'd make a good wife for a timber man.'

She could feel the tide of pink flooding her face and was thankful that Keith was gazing ahead. 'If I knew any.'

'What's wrong with me?' He was teasing her, of course, the light timbre of his tone proved it. She knew he was only speaking in fun, so why did the pain quiver along her nerves? Her thoughts were in a tumult, but fortunately for her peace of mind he didn't appear to expect an answer to his question.

At that moment, to her relief, the bushman left his chain saw and came to stand by the side of the logging truck. The next moment Keith was helping her to the ground and introducing her to his helpers, for the bulldozer driver too had come to join them.

Nicola took to the men at once. She liked their air of relaxation, their quiet way of speaking and engaging grins. But the real reason she warmed to them, she knew, was because they evidently thought a lot of 'the boss'. Indeed, she mused, watching the three as they chatted together, a stranger might find difficulty in distinguishing between employer and bushmen.

'I'm so lucky,' she told the two bushmen as Keith took flasks of hot tea from the truck, 'to come just in time for a cuppa.'

'Only three cups, though,' he was pouring a stream of hot liquid into coloured plastic beakers. 'We weren't expecting to have visitors today.'

'Miss Ayres can have my cup—'

'She's welcome to mine—'

Keith waved the offers aside. 'Nicola will share with me.' The warmth of his look drew her into an intimacy out of all proportion to the light words. 'That is, if you don't mind?'

'Mind?' She caught her breath. If he only knew! She caught her breath, heard herself saying too quickly, too eagerly, 'No, of course not!'

'You first, then.' She took the yellow cup from his hand and their fingers touched.

They talked of ordinary things concerning Keith's work —the ever-present threat of fire, especially through the hot summer months, the need for the lower branches of young trees to be trimmed of growth in order to produce clean straight timber free of knots, the planting of pines close together to make the trees grow tall and straight. It was all of interest to Nicola, but not as interesting as watching Keith's mobile face. He was lounging on a carpet of pine needles and sunshine, filtering through the sombre green of the trees, lighted the planes of his face and burnished the dark hair. Afterwards she climbed back into the truck, watching as one bushman felled the trees and the other drove the bulldozer, while Keith loaded the logs on to the truck. Before she realised the time, an abrupt silence alerted her to the fact that the chain saw had ceased working and with a pang of disappointment she saw that the men had stopped work for their lunch break. She couldn't stay much longer. She had seen them working, watched the way in which they cut and hauled the timber, and she had no excuse to linger. No excuse either, she thought bleakly, for postponing any longer the purpose of her visit. A pity to spoil everything. She waited until Keith climbed back into the truck. As he reached a hand towards the starter, she took a deep breath. 'Wait a minute. There's something I wanted to ask you.'

He turned to face her. His hand, dust-covered, brushed her hair back from her hot forehead. 'Whatever you say. You know how I feel about you.' She was acutely aware of his arm thrown around her shoulders. His nearness was making it harder than ever to say what must be said. 'It's just——' she raised clear blue eyes to his indulgent glance. 'It's about Uncle Walter.'

At once she felt the pressure of his arm around her fall away. Even his voice was different, cold and unresponsive, off-putting. 'Oh, that——'

'Yes, that. You see, there's something troubling me about the whole thing.' The words tumbled from her lips. 'Something that Sharon told me.'

'Sharon?' His tone was sharp, angry, almost accusing. 'What would she know about your uncle?'

Conscious of his dark frown, she wished she had never mentioned the matter. She took a deep breath and endeavoured to speak calmly. 'She came to see me at the cottage today. She was upset about John. Just because we've been a lot together here at the beach, she had this crazy idea that John and I——'

'Don't bother to explain.'

'But there was nothing in it, not in the way she meant,

but try telling her that! She was in such a state, she'd worked herself just about into a nervous wreck. She said she'd be able to make things up with John if I wasn't here, if I went back to England.' She gave an unsteady laugh. 'I think she was trying to get rid of me in a hurry when she told me ...'

'Told you?' Cold steel was in his tone.

It was too late for regrets, she had to go on. 'It was something her father told her years ago. He's died since, but she still remembers——'

'What is it she remembers, Nicola?'

'She—didn't say. She just said I was to ask you about it.' His expression was dark and forbidding and all at once her courage deserted her. 'But when I asked her what she meant she told me she'd made the whole thing up and there was no truth in it at all. She just wanted to annoy me—a sort of revenge, I think she meant. So I told her,' she said slowly, painfully, 'that I had asked you.'

'There's no more to be said in the matter, then, is there?'

He was coldly furious with her, and who could blame him? she thought miserably. She had practically accused him of lying to her. In those first days of her visit when she had stayed at Sky Lodge hadn't he taken the trouble to try to help her discover something about Uncle Walter? He had found old newspapers, looked through family records—well, some of them—without result.

At that moment there came unbidden a memory of a book of family records he had been about to show her, then suddenly he had changed his mind about letting her look through it. But it could have nothing to do with Uncle Walter; it was a record of Keith's family, not hers.

A sneaky glance at the dark closed face made her spirits drop. Stupid, stupid, now she had spoiled it all!

'I'd better be getting back,' she muttered, close to tears, 'the others will be wondering what's happened to me.'

'As you please.' He started the motor and they swung around and took the long dirt track cutting through a sea of pines. They drove on in silence, for what was there to say? When they reached the entrance she said quickly, 'don't trouble to bring the big truck down the driveway.'

'No trouble.' Keith braked outside the cottage and came around the truck to fling open the heavy door. Avoiding his outstretched hand, she dropped to the ground. A swift 'Thanks, Keith' and she had gone without a backward glance. His grim unsmiling face stayed with her as she hurried into the small dwelling and closed the door behind her.

If only she hadn't spoiled everything with her stupid questions! Yet what was there to spoil? For some reason, when she was with him she seemed to forget all about Annabel. Somehow she dismissed the other girl from her mind, as if she didn't exist. It must surely stem from some sort of wishful thinking.

A thought slid into her mind unbidden. Keith hadn't denied what Sharon had told her about him, not really. But then, she reminded herself, he had been much too angry with her for having doubted his word to explain anything.

For Nicola now, time was running out. Wayne had at last ceased to try to persuade her to change her mind about leaving the country, her fictional boy-friend in England had seen to that, but she was guiltily aware of the expression of pain and hopelessness that sat oddly on his bronzed young face.

The telephone call from Annabel came two days before she was due to leave. Gone was the other girl's icy calm, the condescending manner with which she had treated 'the girl from England.' 'A double celebration,' she was saying. 'Surprise, surprise!' You'll hear all about it up at the house tomorrow night! We couldn't leave you out of it all.' Since when, Nicola thought numbly, had she become so important in the scheme of things at Sky Lodge?

She licked dry lips. 'I'm sorry, but I've got an en-gag——'

'See you there, then!' There was a click and the line was dead. It was too late. She had let herself in for the final humiliation, for without a doubt the party would be to announce Annabel's success in winning the Gown of the Year contest and—her heart plunged—a public announcement of Annabel and Keith's approaching wedding. Fix the bright smile on your face, girl, plaster it on hard and fast so it doesn't come off all night!

Indeed, when on the following evening she went with Wayne and Jane into the brightly-lighted hilltop house, no one could have guessed at her heartache.

Annabel made her way through the chattering throng to greet them. A radiant-looking Annabel this, Nicola thought with a pang of the heart. Tonight the other girl looked more attractive than ever in a flowing white off-the-shoulder dress, its only note of colour the arresting border design in a traditional Maori motif. 'So glad you could come,' she cried warmly, 'Keith's around somewhere. Come along and meet everyone!'

At that moment Nicola saw Keith. He was making his way towards them and as their glances locked she was aware of an unspoken message, something she couldn't interpret. The next moment she wrenched her gaze aside. She must have imagined he had tried to tell her something, she thought the next moment, for his tone as he greeted the party was matter-of-fact. 'Glad you made it, Nicola. Hi, Wayne! Jane, you came! There's been a fellow pestering me about you. I got the idea he'd shoot himself if you didn't turn up! Want to put him out of his misery?' He inclined his head and Jane, with a thumbs-up sign over her shoulder, went with him. At that moment the lilt of a pop tune filled the room and presently she and Wayne were joining in the crowd of dancers moving to the insistent beat.

Soon the dance floor was crowded and as the time went by, to Nicola, the heat of the summer night, the chink of glasses at the bar, the music, blurred into a haze. Dancing with Wayne, she caught glimpses of Jane's excited face as she looked up, laughing, towards the extremely tall, thin young man who accompanied her. Annabel appeared to be happy, animated. At Keith she didn't look, it was safer that way.

'Mine, I think?' She was taken by surprise when she found him at her side, tall and erect. As always when he was near, she was aware of a certain heart-stopping quality that was indefinable, and dangerous. Just a dance, she told herself, and a duty one at that. And indeed, he spoke little. Was he still angry with her because she had questioned his motives, as good as told him she didn't believe him? No matter. As they danced in silence, she told herself that if it hadn't been so impossible, almost she might have imagined that he was far from happy tonight, but that of course was ridiculous!

A little later when once again she was dancing with Wayne, she caught sight of Sharon and John on the dance floor. They must have arrived here late, or could the delay have been caused by their making up their differences? she wondered. I wouldn't wonder. For there was no mistaking the expression of happiness on Sharon's face. She danced like a girl in a dream, unaware of anyone else in the room but John. And he—why, he was looking almost fatuously content.

Later on in the evening she was standing alone, Wayne having been drawn away by a group of his friends, when she felt a light touch on her arm. Sharon, but a different Sharon this, an expression of deep happiness in her face, her voice low and assured. 'I just wanted to say I'm sorry. You know? About the other night,' she whispered under cover of the babel around them. 'Those letters I wrote to John—he found them all torn up and stuffed in a shopping bag of his mother's. He would never believe me when I told him I'd written them and he just about hated me for saying that you'd destroyed them. One good thing, though, we've got everything out in the open again and things are just like they were before—even this, look——' She flashed a hand before Nicola's and a solitaire diamond winked in the light. 'I'm truly sorry for what I said, honestly, Nicola.'

'It' all right,' Nicola smiled. 'It wasn't all that much fun for me, being with John. Not when he had you on his mind all the time.'

Sharon said quickly, 'Thank heaven I was in time to tell you how sorry I am—there's John looking for me, I've got to go!'

Vaguely, through her heartache, Nicola realised that a group was forming at the end of the room, a laughing crowd surrounding Keith and Annabel. Wayne, once more back with her, handed her a glass of champagne from a tray a waiter was passing around. 'Now for the big announcement!'

A sudden hush fell over the crowded room, then Keith's deep voice reached her. Nicola took a deep breath and braced herself for the announcement he was about to make. 'Just a celebration tonight, to mark the occasion ... proud to announce that Annabel has won the Gown of the Year award for dress design. You can see the gown right here this evening.' He held his goblet high. 'To Annabel, may this be just the start of success.'

'To Annabel!' The toast was drunk and afterwards there was the sound of stamping feet and the thunder of applause.

Annabel took the acclaim smilingly. 'Thank you, everyone, but don't go away yet! I've got another announcement to make, something a lot more important than the fashion award, at least it is to me!'

Suddenly Nicola felt a little sick. She had thought she could take it, the news of Keith and Annabel's approaching wedding date, but now ... she glanced wildly around her. At the edge of the crowd where she and Wayne were standing, she wasn't far from the door. If she could slip away now she might be able to make her way to Keith's study. What was it Sharon had cried: 'Why don't you ask Keith Lorimer to show you the family album?' It was a chance she might not have again, with everyone gathered here in the room.

Coward! a voice deep in her mind jeered, you only want to escape.

No matter. She was very pale. 'Wayne, I feel a bit ... funny. I'll be back in a minute or so.'

Instantly he was filled with concern. 'You look as white as a sheet,' he whispered. 'Let me take you outside for some fresh air.'

'No, no,' she was frantic now, 'I know where the guest room is. I left some headache tablets there. I won't be long.'

Cutting short his anxious efforts to be of some assistance, she hurried away. She couldn't have chosen a better time. Her footfall was silent on the carpeted floor as she turned into the dining room, ran along a passage and reached the lounge room.

Swiftly she closed the door behind her and felt for the light switch. As the room was flooded with light, she glanced swiftly around her. How well she remembered Keith taking the bound volume from the sideboard and later, placing it in the desk, *without showing her the contents*. What was it she had said or done that had impelled him to change his mind? Her thoughts raced as she moved towards the desk. What if it were locked? But it opened to her touch and the big hard-covered book with its bulging clippings was in plain view.

She riffled through the pages. If only she had more time, and knew what it was she was searching for. A name? A date? All at once the black printed headlines of a newspaper cutting sprang to meet her gaze.

HEROIC RESCUE ENDS IN TRAGEDY.

Walter de Serville—but that was Uncle Walter's name—well, part of it. She bent over the faded newspaper clipping, scanning the paragraphs and taking in whole sentences at a glance.

'Walter de Serville, a recent arrival in the town, was one of a party of picnickers by the river yesterday when a small boy who had slipped away from the group was seen to be clinging to a ledge half way up the rock face. Mr de Serville volunteered to rescue the child and he had almost gained the top of the cliff and had already thrown the boy to safety, when he missed his footing and fell to the rocks

*beneath. A doctor was sent for, but he verified that death
had been instantaneous, resulting from serious head in-
juries*

*It is understood that efforts are being made to locate
Mr de Serville's next of kin.'*

Her bemused gaze went to a small newspaper clipping.
*Will any person knowing the whereabouts of Walter de
Serville, believed to be late of Western Australia, kindly
communicate with the following address.*

She turned a page and there, smiling up at her with his
rakish grin, was Uncle Walter's face, the likeness was unmistakable. But why had he changed his name? A letter
from the Police Department in Perth, addressed to Mr
Henry Lorimer, Waihi—that would be Keith's father—
spelled out the answer only too clearly.

'Regarding your enquiries concerning Walter de Serville,
we have reason to believe that this man, under the name
of Walter de Serville Fletcher, is wanted for questioning
by our department in the matter of an attempted hold-up
on a bank in an outlying district. A photograph is enclosed and we would be glad of any information you could
supply in connection with this matter.' She could see no
further for the mist in her eyes.

'So—you know——'

Intent on her discoveries, she hadn't heard the door
open. Guiltily she turned to face Keith's cool glance. If
only *he* hadn't been the one to catch her out!

He came to stand beside her.

'You knew, didn't you?' she whispered. 'The moment
I said the name was de Serville, you knew all about Uncle
Walter. Why didn't you tell me?'

'And spoil all those illusions of yours? Put a burden on
that aunt you think so much of? Hell, I thought, I'll let her
go back to England without knowing all this. It wouldn't
do any good, her knowing what had happened, and it
could cause her a heck of a lot of heartache.'

She said very low, 'You could have told me about the
rescue. It was a wonderful thing that he did.'

'Do you think I don't know that!' His voice roughened.

'Why do you think all these cuttings are kept here? That kid, the boy your uncle rescued all those years ago, happened to be myself!'

She stared up at him, eyes wide with surprise, 'You!' An unwilling smile curved her lips. 'That figures. I can just imagine you as a small boy, climbing cliffs, getting away from everyone and doing what you wanted to.'

'Can you?' His voice had the old tenderness that turned her bones to water. 'It was a bad business, that, not being able to find anyone belonging to him. My dad told me that he tried every avenue he could think of to get in touch with relatives and then in the end he made enquiries over in Western Australia—someone remembered your uncle saying that he'd come from there to Waihi. A reply came from the Police Department in Perth and that was one letter my dad didn't answer.' All at once his voice was gentle. 'Don't feel too badly about it.'

'I don't!' Nicola said with spirit. 'I think he was wonderful! I'm ever so proud of him—Oh, I know it was pretty awful, what happened over in Australia, but he didn't hurt anyone, he didn't even get away with anything, and whatever it was that he did, he made up for it all in the end.'

'Just what I've been trying to tell you.'

'And that was why he changed his name?' She was speaking her thoughts aloud.

He nodded. 'It was common enough in those days for a man who, for one reason or another, wanted to start afresh in a new country. Easy too, there was no check on passenger lists of boats sailing between here and Australia and a man could get a ticket under any old name he chose.'

She was scarcely listening; an astounding thought was creeping through her mind. 'But that means that if it hadn't been for Uncle Walter, you might not be here.'

His voice was very soft. 'Would it matter to you?'

'*Would it matter?*' Too late she realised that her unthinking response to her question, the telltale expression of her face, had betrayed her. Useless now to lie and preof her face, had betrayed her. Useless now to lie and pretend. Keith had stepped close to her, his hands cupping her face. 'Tell me, would you care, my darling?'

She couldn't fight any longer against the truth. Could it be because she was leaving him for ever that nothing seemed to matter any more? She heard her own voice, low and tremulous. 'You know it would.'

'You must know I love you.' Surely she must be dreaming?—for only in dreams could this be happening. Even in the dream, though, some semblance of sanity prevailed. She wrenched herself free. 'How can you say that, *how can you*, when you and Annabel—' There, the words were out. Reckless now, she was beyond caring. All she knew was that she was finished with subterfuge and lies.

'Me—and Annabel?' Disbelief mingled with bewilderment in his tone, then suddenly he gave a great shout of sheer exuberance. 'Is that what's been on your mind all this time? You actually imagined that Annabel and I—'

She stared up at him, afraid to trust the joyousness of his expression. Surely a man who had something to hide wouldn't look like that? 'It was just,' she faltered, 'that everyone told me that you and she—'

'Everyone should mind their own business.'

'And then,' she glanced away, unable to sustain his brilliant gaze, 'that night when I first arrived here and you showed me the plans for your home. I took it you were going to modernise Sky Lodge and live here...with Annabel.'

'Nicola, my foolish little one!' He took her in his arms and then very gently, his lips found hers. 'There's only one girl I want to marry. If only I'd known,' the words were whispered between kisses, 'I could have straightened it all out in a couple of minutes. The plans we were working on that night you were here were for the modernising of a block of shops with living quarters, including a boutique that Annabel's planning to run, right here in the main street. I'm financing the venture and she's pretty certain that her exclusive dress shop will go along like wildfire, especially now that she'll have a good business light in his eyes made her spirits soar. 'You didn't know about her partner, did you? Tony's away on the Continent right now, picking up fashion ideas, but he'll be back in time to see the start of the new shopping block. They'll make a good team,' he grinned, 'a husband and wife team as well. If you hadn't taken off a few minutes ago you would have heard the announcement Annabel was making, wedding plans and all! But, man,' he gave a great sigh of relief, 'am I glad you did!' His voice softened, deepened. 'I love you so. You must have guessed. Sometimes I even hoped——'

'I know, I know, I felt the same way. I tried not to, but all the time——'

He held her at arm's length, taking in her flushed cheeks and tousled hair. 'It's for always my darling, you know, don't you?' Once again she was caught close to his muscular chest. 'I'll never let you go, not even to go back home to tell your folks. To come so close to losing you,' he muttered hoarsely, 'and now——' Tenderness merged with passion and desire as he kissed her once again and it was a long time later when Nicola pushed the hair back from her flushed face.

'Wayne!' she spoke as if in a dream. 'He'll be wondering what's happened to me. I told him,' she explained guiltily, 'that I wasn't feeling well and that,' she twinkled up at him, 'is just about the understatement of the year!'

'He'll never go for that story,' his gaze was on her radiant face, 'not the way you look right at this moment.'

'He'll have to take my word for it——' She broke off as the door was flung open and Wayne hurried towards her. Her heart smote her at his concerned expression. 'Nicola! Are you feeling all right?' The next moment, aware of her excited look and Keith's smiling face, he stood still. He took the blow well, Nicola thought. 'I get it. I guess I might have known how things were.' His twisted smile was a long way from amusement. 'That guy you were crazy about, the one who meant the whole world to you, with the moon and stars thrown in, he wasn't way over in England, he was right here?'

Nicola was feeling so blissfully happy she wanted everyone else to share in her joy, especially Wayne. She sought for words to soften the blow and said inadequately, 'It just—happened.'

'Don't tell me!' Once again he gave the twisted grin that sat oddly on his open young face. 'Don't I know it! Anyway,' with an effort he pulled himself together, 'here's wishing you both all the best for the future.'

'Thanks, mate.' Keith wrung Wayne's hand with vigour.

To Nicola Wayne said on a sigh, 'Guess I won't be driving you to Auckland to catch the London-bound plane tomorrow after all?' He swallowed, squared his shoulders, and left them alone.

Nicola felt such a tide of happiness surge over her that it was only with an effort she forced herself to think of anything or anyone else but Keith. 'I'll have to ring through to Aunt in the morning and tell her the news.'

'You can tell her,' his gaze resting on her flushed face, was deep and intent, 'that the wedding's going to be next month and she'll have to get cracking and get herself some summer gear for herself and book a trip out here for the big day. How about putting a call through now?'

'This minute?'

'Why not? Midnight here means it'll be near enough to midday over there. Look, what's the phone number?'

Nicola told him, watching him as he picked up the receiver and dialled an international call. Could this scene really be taking place, all these wonderful things happening at once? Her mind was in a tumult of excitement as Keith handed her the receiver.

'Is that you, Nicola? Aunt Bella's light tones came through as clearly as though she were in the room beside them. 'Are you all right, dear?'

'Oh yes, yes!' I'm so excited I don't know how to tell you——'

'Tell me what, love? You haven't found Uncle Walter, have you?'

'Uncle Walter? Heavens, no! I'll tell you all about that

later. It's Keith——' His nearness was sending her thoughts whirling.

'Let me.' He took the receiver and the next moment his strong tones rang out. 'That's right, Aunt Bella—I think I'm entitled to call you aunt. The thing is, I want to marry your niece. We've just decided about it ourselves.'

Laughing, Nicola took the receiver once again. 'So I won't be on the plane this week as I'd planned——'

'I understand, love. He does sound very nice! Masterful, but nice!'

Nicola giggled. 'You have no idea! You'll be meeting him soon. We want you to come out here for the wedding next month. I know it's awfully short notice for you to make the arrangements——'

'Nonsense, child. I have a telephone, and one perfectly sound leg! This call must be costing you a fortune ...' Nicola didn't catch the rest of the words for Keith was saying swiftly, 'Tell her to get a single air ticket. If she's on her own over there she might find she likes the place and decide to stay on here for good.'

'Keith says to tell you——'

'I know—I heard him. Just what I was thinking myself—but it's nice to know you're wanted. I'm so pleased you're so happy, love. Goodbye!'

In the sudden silence, Nicola replaced the receiver. She said slowly, 'She seems quite taken with the idea of coming out here for keeps. It doesn't take long for Aunt Bella to make up her mind. She said to tell you that it's nice to be wanted.'

'You should know!' Keith's deep intent glance sent her pulses leaping, then everything else slipped from her mind in the heady rapture of his kiss.

Harlequin Presents...

Romance novels that speak
the language of love known to
women the world over.

Harlequin Presents...

A distinctive series of dramatic
love stories created
especially for you
by world-acclaimed
authors.

HARLEQUIN SUPERROMANCE

A Contemporary Love Story

Complete and mail this coupon today!

Harlequin Reader Service

In U.S.A.
MPO Box 707
Niagara Falls, NY 14302

In Canada
649 Ontario St.
Stratford, Ont. N5A 6W2

Please send me END OF INNOCENCE,
HARLEQUIN SUPERROMANCE #1. I am enclosing my
check or money order for $2.25 for each copy ordered.

Number of copies _____ @ $2.25 each
                                    = $_____

Please send me LOVE'S EMERALD FLAME,
HARLEQUIN SUPERROMANCE #2. I am enclosing my
check or money order for $2.25 for each copy ordered.

Number of copies _____ @ $2.25 each
                                    = $_____

Total $_____

N.Y. and Ariz. residents add appropriate sales
                                      tax $_____

Postage and handling $_____.59_____

Final total $_____

I enclose _____
(Please send check or money order. We cannot be responsible for
cash sent through the mail.)
Prices subject to change without notice.

NAME_____
                        (Please Print)
ADDRESS_____

CITY_____

STATE/PROV._____ZIP/POSTAL CODE_____

Offer expires May 31, 1981   101563323